TASTING ROOM CONFIDENTIAL

JENNIFER LUCK MULLER

ADVANCED PRAISE FOR TASTING ROOM CONFIDENTIAL

"A must read before visiting the area."

"One quirky woman's re-coming of age story, set in wine country."

"This behind-the-vines view is a cultural gem, revealing the truths of winery tasting rooms."

"Muller details some of her personal life and quirky reflections, including how to behave at tasting rooms. She explains how tasting rooms function during the busy and off seasons and about the various pet peeves of wine industry workers. Also, she famously advises customers to try the merlot (it needs a comeback!)."

"Tasting rooms have many dynamics at play, and this book reveals components of those sipping wine next to you. This book also made me laugh out loud at the absurdity and audacity found in the patrons of Paso."

"Structured as a loose collection of humorous anecdotes, Tasting Room Confidential is equal parts confessional narrative and industry commentary on winery tasting rooms."

"Released in 2026 to wide acclaim, the book is destined to be a piece of cultural anthropology. It's both an autobiographical fiction novel and an unfiltered look at the aspects of high-end tasting rooms in Paso Robles wine country. The author describes them through her lens of curiosity, and the personal lives of those working there who really care about crafting an experience for patrons. Muller believes that the tasting room is no place for distracting aromas or disrespect. This book is not only for those with a reverence for wine, but for all who are curious about human behavior while drinking fine wine and for those interested in experiencing this area of California for themselves."

"Best read with a glass of red in your hand."

ABOUT THE AUTHOR

Jennifer Luck Muller, M.Ed., is at her heart, an educator. Her professional background involved work as an education consultant, in communications as well as non-profit sectors. She loves conversations that make her feel like she's learning the truth about someone, always roots for the underdog, and seeks out stories that are inspiring. This book is the result of her creativity and experiences from her profession in hospitality as a Wine Educator at winery tasting rooms in Paso Robles' wine country. Currently working on her next book, Jennifer calls San Luis Obispo County California her home. When not writing with a cat on her lap, she's soaking up time with her family and is likely sitting poolside with her pup, while sipping a really wonderful glass of local zinfandel.

This book was able to reach its fullest potential thanks to the following: My beta reader, Dr. Elisa S. Feingold; Novelist and Professor of Screenwriting Ms. Carrie Newell Lacina; and Mrs. Mindy T. Conde of The Crimson Quill Editing Services.

Out of respect for people's privacy, I have changed the names of most individuals, and those without pseudonyms have given me permission to use their name and likeness.

Written in California.

Cover design by Peter Gend

Author photo by Andy Hardeman

ISBN: 979-8-9941965-6-4

Dedicated to my marvelous parents who have always encouraged me, my son Leland whom I love to infinity and beyond, and to the sensational man at the end of the bar whose first proposal came when I poured him a splash of a Cabernet.

THE BEGINNING

I wanted a job in customer service. I imagined a part time job in customer service would change my life for the better. I had nothing to lose. I dreamed of working in customer service. I dreamed of being thanked for my efforts pouring drinks. I dreamed of having a lunch break in which no one needed anything from me for a whole 20 minutes while I listened to an audiobook and ate leftovers out of a piece of plasticware. My people-pleasing nature dreamed of getting instant gratification for my skills and kindness when I received a smile, 'thank you,' or cash tip. I dreamed of meeting adults, being heard and hearing them.

I had worked on myself in a big way over the past year. In 2018 I was working out to get lean and lose the baby weight. My partner said we could give our son a sibling, after I lost the weight. While I was working to make my body smaller, my confidence was getting bigger. When my partner changed his mind after my 80-pound weight loss, I felt an all-time high/low. Happy that I reached my goal, and sad that my family wouldn't be expanding. Since I couldn't gift a sibling to my son, I felt like I should do something else with my toned physique, I wanted to test-drive my new body and newfound confidence in the real world. Like with real adults, doing a real job. I searched Craigslist's Job Opportunities section and found a bar hiring for a bartender. It was at a beer bar I had been to before; in fact, the growler bottles were displayed on my rustic open-shelved kitchen. The job checked all the boxes. It was so close to my house, I could even ride my bike there, further encouraging my fitness goals as well. It was a tad over minimum wage so I felt they respected humans. I applied and interviewed the next week. To prepare for my interview, I composed my Word document resume, was on time, and answered the questions pleasantly. I soon learned I was ill-equipped. The man interviewing me, the owner, said they wanted a certified Cicerone working there. I didn't know what that meant at the time, so the teacher in me can explain it to you now:

A Cicerone is the title one earns after proving they're an expert in the brewing, pairing, and serving of all varieties of beer. The Cicerone training proves one is a true professional in the hospitality and alcoholic beverage industry.

Well, that certainly wasn't on the job posting, if I remembered right. Plus, it's not like it was something I didn't feel I could learn. I considered myself a quick-learner, and not just one who used that buzzword on resumes, for I had graduated from a California Ivy League school and went on to earn my Master's Degree in Education, to boot. Plus, the few years prior, I had toured the Miller Lite Brewery in Milwaukee Wisconsin. Isn't that enough? Plus, I have German heritage — the land of beer would run through my veins and aid in my knowledge. All that paired with my confidence gained from earning my degrees, I felt I could certainly learn to truly love beer. I could notice its nuances and learn to properly pour from a keg. I knew I could rise to the challenge, but after seeing the rough state of the bar in daylight, the juxtaposition of wanting someone highly skilled in beer working at a rural biker bar was odd. Given the well-lit vibe of the place, I expected big muscles, tattoos, and motorcycle driver's licenses were more important than certified brains when working there. Maybe he interviewed me because when I said I could ride my bike there, he assumed motorbike, not a vintage Schwinn. The interviewer, Mr. Bardun, was a nice enough man, but he must not have seen my deftness for learning new skills or my inclination to the industry, because he did not end up hiring me.

Well, that one decision helped set into motion a series of events where I realized tending to a bar of some sort would match my personality bubbliness, but perhaps I was better suited to a place that was a *tad* more elegant. And, as I had learned, a place willing to train on the job. Back to Craigslist I went as this was 2019, remember. In the same Job Opportunity category, Customer Service, I saw the listing for Stonefruit Canyon Winery. Their requirements were minimal, stating weekend availability a must and it wasn't too-too far from home, so I decided to give it a try. I could ask my son's dad to watch our son on weekends when he wasn't working on his IT business. I adjusted my resume, making the Education section in bigger font, to highlight my advanced degrees after my experience with Mr. Bardun made me realize I needed to prove I was a quick-learner, and then applied. Then, if luck would have it, hopefully I would get an interview. It was listed in the Job Opportunity section after all, and I took it a tad literally and wanted the opportunity to change my life for the better — it was an opportunity after all. I knew it would be humbling at times, but I was okay with that sensation as I expected it when exiting my comfort zone. I wanted a chance to make my life better. Because, hell, even an interview was a chance. In 2019, I wanted a lot of chances. A chance to dress up in clothes that command attention, and command respect. A chance to learn something as sexy-sounding as wine tasting, and be a part of the revered California wine industry.

I began by tweaking my resume a bit. I had been working as a tutor for college students for the past fifteen years. It's pretty unique to say that I had been essentially 'in college' since I was eighteen but only six years were just for me. I also wanted to give written credit on my credentials to the being that took the most space in my heart — my son. I used the term Housewife Extraordinaire, to imply that I was good at serving others and that's exactly how I see the hospitality industry.

The interview was at ten am in the tasting room about 20 minutes north of my home. After driving there with the radio playing Raffi, you know the hippie who sang songs for the children of the 1980s and that I shared with my young son. I knew I was so in my head about this interview that I forgot to adjust the radio to my own station. I was so used to my car being in Mommy Mobile Mode. So, I arrived and parked my yellow Toyota in the bumpy dirt parking lot. On my passenger seat, I had my black faux-leather notepad holder with extra resumes tucked inside. I went into the tasting room and was quickly escorted to a back room. A black folding chair was pointed out to me, and I sat on it across from two chair backs. The people in the chairs cinematically spun around and faced me after I was already seated. I had seen this move in a movie, but in real life it was quite a way to make an entrance. One by one they introduced themselves remaining seated and giving low eye contact saying they were the Wine Club Manager Rhonda and the Tasting Room Manager Tom.

They sat across from me and I noticed her wearing a drapey grey cardigan, maroon denim-like pants and tall sheepskin boots. More Bear Claw than Ugg based on the fraying stitches. He had on a fitted off-brand polo shirt and slim fit indigo wash jeans. Out from his intentionally too-short pants popped colorful socks. I take them in and think to myself, a Fun Sock Guy and Cozy Girl types I've met before. After settling in my seat a moment longer, I notice it was quite a cold area and adjacent to the wine cellar as I could see the boxes stacked upon each other and knew there was wine in there from my visits to BevMo. I knew wine fridges existed, thanks to browsing Costco, and knew where wine was kept had to be cold, to keep the wine fresh. I wasn't surprised to feel the cold air coming through the door onto my legs popping down and out from my brown corduroy skirt. But I was surprised by how okay they were with the chill. Reminding myself of my goal, and again, equipped with my resume and high hopes, I sat lady-like in my interview with a desire to please them. I really wanted the job. I really wanted to feel like a whole person again. I wanted to eat lunch on my break and actually taste my food and not just eat something my toddler refused to eat today even though it was a favorite last week. I wanted to stand at the bar and pour drinks for people who would say "thank you" to me. A real genuine "thank you" would begin to make me feel useful, and that my usefulness was appreciated. My dream of landing a job in Customer Service could come to fruition if I played my cards right. I wanted this opportunity because it would be good to be around different types of people I could learn to serve. The reality set in while I sat on that cold chair. I had to ace this interview to make my dream come true. So, when they asked a question about wine, and I found a chance to mention my favorite wine was, Ask Me Nicely from Cellar 420. Now, when you say, "Ask Me Nicely" it most definitely sounds like "ax me nicely" especially when you see the picture of a giant wooden ax ominously over a person's face; a cartoony rendition of Munch's The Scream on the bottle's label. My taste for wine was amateur at best and that wine was definitely some-thing my date had bought at a grocery store or mini market. This Ask Me Nicely wine truly was the first wine that I enjoyed. Years ago, I had been on a date at the beach, and maybe it was my company, or the sunset enhancing the sips, but I did really like that wine. Plus, because my date was proud to tell me, "It's local," I felt it worth mentioning during my interview here in

Paso. Gosh, I wish I had another type of wine I liked, or could pretend I liked. That would have a better, well, easier to articulate name. I suddenly panicked inside, wondering if they thought I was asking to be hurt during this interview, but a rush of relief traveled through me as I figured out, they didn't think that at all during my interview. Phew! Thankfully, Tom and Rhonda were familiar with the Cellar 420 brand and knew its labels pushed the envelope of being proper. In fact, the wine world was small around here. They told me how their bosses had actually begun that winery years back, and it was on local store shelves all the time.

Tom took the lead in the interview as he said I would be working for him. The questions were simple, what days and times would I be willing to work, and if was I comfortable talking to different types of people. He said the word "different" in a way that sounded like he wanted to use mouthwash after simply saying the word, as if his interactions with the people were less than desirable. The questions then quickly got abstract. "What would you do with $1,000,000 if you could do anything?" he asked. "I would start a good news website or even blog, in which I only highlighted good news from around the world," I confidently replied. "What's your favorite band?" Tom followed up.

"311. They were popular in the '90's but actually are still around. It's neat their fans still love them," I replied wistfully. "What was your last job like?" Tom asked. "Like, oh, do you mean what did I *do*?" I asked Tom.

"No, what were *they* like?" He repeated, thinking he was clarifying, as he quickly blinked and narrowed his eyes in what I read as annoyance. I turned to Rhonda, made eye contact with her, then turned my gaze back to Tom and said, "they were nice." And took the chance to speak about what I wanted to talk about instead. Diverting, I said, "Having my son really changed my ability to work as I didn't have reliable childcare." I trailed off, "his dad works a lot, and my son is young and needs mom. My folks moved to Atascadero recently, and they're thrilled to babysit him while I'm at work. Most of my jobs in the past two years were online, like from home. That's kind of why I want this job. I want to have an in-person job in Customer Service where I can use my quick learning skills, and knowledge of the Central Coast to help show it off to visitors."

Ah, I breathed a sigh of relief. I was glad I could get all that out and explain myself. But the panic set in again when Tom did the blinky thing and said, "Show it off?" Tom questioned. Turning to Rhonda again looking for a clue from her about this guy Tom. I sensed she was used to this and I hoped her comfort meant he was safe. Before replying, I said, "Yeah, the Central Coast. It's so pretty here. I love taking little hikes and exploring different parks and views in North County now. I used to live in South County."

But the tension from Tom was palpable so I cut myself short. I hadn't socialized with adults much, but his eye thing was either a tic like in Tourette's or something boys did in middle school when we had to pass papers out to their other classmates and looking at their peers was partially required. I wasn't sure how to understand him and felt inadequate, at least socially, when talking to him. Had my social skills really declined as I spoke to a toddler all day? I hoped not! Although I was not sure what to think, I was sure of one thing. I definitely knew it was good Rhonda worked there too, as she seemed to understand his awkward vibes and her willingness to work with him showed that I could probably manage it also. Without her presence, I likely wouldn't have wanted the job in that particular space as the cold and socially awkward working environment was too much like what I was trying to get myself out of. I had to remind myself why I wanted this job to change my life. I wanted to continue to change myself and change my life, my future. I had spent the year before at a gym lifting barbells to better myself and my future, and I was hoping for the same dopamine rush behind the tasting room bar.

At what was thankfully becoming the end of the interview, Tom prompted Rhonda to ask a question too. Rhonda didn't seem prepared for this. She seemed a bit flustered. As she was put on the spot, paused a moment, gazed at my cover letter and resume and asked a two-part question. She asked, "What does it mean on your resume when you say, 'housewife extraordinaire,' and what is the name of your dog?" A sigh of relief came over me as I felt thankful someone looked at the resume, I had worked so hard on, but I never imagined my dog's name choice may affect my ability to get this job. I stopped looking down at my platform loafers and looked up and smiled. Another random-feeling set of questions, but these I could answer. I breathed out, realizing I was holding my breath for far too long, and began to answer her questions. I said, "My dog is a goldendoodle, she's 2. Her name is Luna, because she's white and bright, like the moon." I continued on explaining that the Housewife Extraordinaire part was pointing to the fact that I wasn't employed out of the home in about four years. Sure, I had worked a lot online tutoring and managing social media accounts for small local businesses, and felt putting all the work I do as a housewife and mother was super relevant to a customer service job. Because anyone who's been in the toughest 'hood there is, motherhood, knows it is essentially serving and cleaning up after others. My son's dad worked so many hours a day building up his IT business and often spent all of his waking hours in his home office. I was happy to deliver him warm coffee and leave homemade lunches at his door so I wouldn't distract him and instead help him grow his business. To lessen his load, I also took on all the housework with full enthusiasm. I liked working from home and working at home, for describing women who clean and run a house as 'not working' is surely one of the most successful conspiracies of the 20th century.

After I answered Rhonda, Tom abruptly said, "Ok thanks! Bye! Josh will show you to the front." Startled by the abruptness of it all, I felt I said something wrong. I stood up, smoothed out my blouse that was tucked in, and reached my right hand out to shake their hands. Tom's right hand was already between us, waiting for me to finish fixing myself up. I shook it, then Rhonda's. I turned to see Josh already in the doorway behind me. I quickly thought that maybe he'd communicated to Tom in the doorway somehow, but suddenly wondered if he standing there the whole time? I wondered, and wondered, but quickly stopped having any thoughts whatsoever in my head when Josh smiled. What a smile it was. I felt this smile wasn't for me. It's the kind of smile that could take down a concert stadium full of giddy girls, it was that big and charismatic. Getting back to myself, I continued being ushered to walk up the ramp and into the kitchen past him. Then, as if assuming Tom's decision to get me out of there, he walked faster to lead me out of the bar area.

I was now completely baffled by myself, again. Maybe something like: Amidst my confusion over the odd turns the interview had taken, Josh's kind smiles pointed my way as he guided me outside had me baffled by myself in a new way. First of all, I was in a committed relationship and didn't think I'd even be a giddy girl whose heart would turn to mush ever again. I felt something in me I hadn't felt for a long time- attraction. And confusion. What had I said wrong during the interview? I walked outside to my sub-compact hatchback car, and gathered myself. I looked at the rolling hills, and beautiful bucolic atmosphere. I noticed other wineries in the distance. *What had just happened? What did I do wrong and what would I do better?* I asked myself while looking at the other wineries truly helped calm me, because at this point, I thought I had really messed up my interview and realized that if I couldn't get a job here, there were other options. Other opportunities for me to listen to the tug in me that said I would be good at this, and perhaps I just needed some perseverance and someday someone would see that I would fit in customer service too.

After leaving the interview, I did what most millennial women would do if given childcare and 20 minutes to herself — I pulled out of the tasting room driveway and drove the mile and a half to Target. I justified the stop by thinking how this was prudent and how I wanted to combine my driving trips to make the gas usage worth it. Plus, having a few more moments to myself while getting something on my shopping list before going home, would make today feel like a win even though I had my doubts about my interview at Stonefruit Canyon.

When browsing Women's Accessories, I received a phone call. That's news in itself as my phone hardly ever works due to the cell phone scramblers in the store. But it did work that day. The first real miracle of that day. It was an 805 number and I wondered if I had left something during the interview, as it was odd to get a call within the first half hour of leaving the interview. So, I answered the call as I stood by the sunglasses display. It was Tom, and he was offering me the job and hoping I could start next week. Wow, what a quick surprise! I mean, I knew I could do the job and learn everything, but I was surprised by how quickly he called me with the offer. It was Monday, and he wanted me to start by Thursday. That was a mere four days to learn things as Saturday was Zinfandel Weekend in Paso Robles and the winery was expected to be very busy. After agreeing to the job, we decided I would start Wednesday and we hung up. A mere three days then. I stood there with the sunglasses in my hand and looked at myself in the mirror. I put the very colorful but flimsy feeling sunglasses on and cocked my head to the side, the way a golden retriever does when it is thinking. I stood in the mirror. Despite the fingerprints on the mirror, I could see my face clearly as the little fingers couldn't reach that high. I looked and saw myself in a new way. I was an employed woman. With this big impending change and this real dream coming true, I looked at myself differently. Maybe it was the sunglasses, as cute sunglasses can make a big difference when styling, but I truly felt empowered in that moment. Little by little, I was making my own dreams come true. I was able to change my life, and here I was doing it.

IT'S MY FIRST DAY

To prepare for my first shift, I spent hours scrolling and perusing the Stonefruit Canyon website. I read how the wine was described and looked at Pinterest for outfits to wear to a winery for wine tasting. I went into my first shift and I felt my dream was coming true. I didn't have a big felt hat like the girls on Pinterest, but I did have a fun going out top. I got dressed in what I call, "outside clothes" meaning not "home clothes" which tended to have remnants of motherhood on them. I had glimpses of the real world I remembered from long ago. My jeans still fit, which was a surprise as I hadn't needed to wear actual pants in what felt like forever. Stretchy pants from Lularoe and Target fit my work-from-home and motherhood lifestyle just fine. My jeans and top paired well my favorite maroon sweater nicely. My going out top may make me too cold, and since I remember the interview room being chilly, I brought the sweater. I wondered, if this ephemera would be enough to make me feel like I'd made it. Chasing a similar feeling to the one I had when I tried on the sunglasses after the call in Target. Paired with my outside clothes, and a lunch packed in one of those little plastic rectangle containers that processed lunch meat sometimes comes in, I was ready. Being a daughter of an immigrant, I wasn't fearful of new things. It was in my blood. With sensible shoes on my feet, for supported standing and lifting heavy things all day, I headed out. I felt full of hope; it felt so dang good.

When I arrived, I went into the tasting room and I officially met my new coworker, Josh. Talking with someone 10 years younger and in a different phase of life was refreshing. There was something kindred about him. I wanted to feel free — as free as he seemed to be. Free like I could reinvent myself into something new. I wanted to be new. I was brave and ready to take flight. When I had doubts that I actually wasn't ready, I reminded myself I only had to make it to lunch time and could find peace in my car while eating a lunch and looking out onto the vineyards. Vineyards sure have a way to get Romantics daydreaming, don't they? I was a day-dreamer and felt an exuberant giddiness simply thinking that this was the beginning of my new life. I knew it was big.

Preparing myself for something new, I reminded myself the wine tasting room is a job of education, and having earned a master's degree in teaching years ago, I felt I could transition to the role perfectly. I was convincing myself this would be enough to feel confident and that was reinforced when Josh began his official training by saying, "One thing you may have noticed about wine is that the tasting room experience is much different than selecting a bottle from the shelf at a grocery store. The tasting room's wine professionals have an immense effect on the enjoyment of the wine. Hence the name we sometimes have: Wine Educator." When he said that we're even called educators, I thought to myself, *I will absolutely fit in.* I listened to him and admittedly ogled at his crooked smile getting lost in not knowing how to reconcile this distraction within myself. Josh continued, "We point out the history of the grapes, the vineyard's struggles and joys and the flavors they impose along with the winery's enologist's interpretation of the wine's flavor."

I didn't know what an enologist was, but it sounded cool and sciencey.

"But also, it depends on you, you see. No pressure!" he said as he chuckled with that smile that I decided could simultaneously calm and excite just about any woman with a heartbeat. "The connections made during the tasting experience can make or break a sale, just as one's breakfast choices can affect flavors left on the taste bud when arriving to an 11am tasting appointment after your coffee filled breakfast. When the pourer connects with the patron, magic can happen. The dialogue and connection come between sips. Want to give it a try? I see people just arrived in the parking lot right now."

I offered to watch the first one. He nodded, and said, "Okay, one last thing, then... through the sips, the flavor of the wine can instantly be delicious, insanely delicious, or it can be a flop. All because of the exchange in mannerisms and dialogue. Let's be honest, if they want to drink alcohol, they can do that at home, but there's something that calls you to drink alcohol in public." I learned that this place puts the *social* in social drinking, it can also be notably the guaranteed fun part of drinking in public with others. Similarly, going out to dinner and chatting with the waitress, is like how it is to be welcomed and acquainted with the place, wine tasting rooms serve a similar function — connection." Noted. The now nerdy-sounding Josh points out further, "The job of a restaurant's sommelier is to pair one of the wines to your meal selection. They also take into account your preferences and how many people are at the table. If there's a larger group, they may suggest two wines. One for appetizer and salad courses and one with dinner. This would give each person at the table two half glasses of wine and allow for a more crowd-pleasing dining experience as there always seems to be one person at the table who prefers white wine over red wine, despite the traditional pairing suggestions. An even larger number of people at a table can allow for a third bottle as some people like a dessert wine like a port as the ending to their meal."

The boy could talk, and I hadn't even heard him mention any of the specific things we do, how we handle the glasses, or pour the wine, or even anything about the wine. He didn't say a word about the chardonnay or zinfandels listed on the menus laying on the top of the bar. I fretted that it wasn't part of the training as maybe I should have known about this already. As he spoke, I couldn't take my eyes off his mouth. He talked fast, and was so assured of himself. Where did his confidence come from, I wondered. We both looked out to the parking lot, and after noticing the group getting closer to the front door, he said, "They're coming in, are you ready? Watch this."

I TRUST HIM ALREADY

J ust as I was watching a customer through the glass door as he grabs the door handle to swing the door open for him and his fellow guests, Samantha summoned me into the kitchen. With her gentle, "come here" hand motion, I left my training and met Samantha in the kitchen. She asks me, "Hey, did you bring in your driver's license and social security card? We need to fill out the new hire paperwork."

"Of course!" I answered, and went to my bag which I had placed in the back room. She made copies of the documents, and added them to my employee file. While the copy machine was shooting its lightening strobe left and right as it copied my proof of being born and being a driver, she asked about my dog Luna, "Does Luna like dog parks? I just took my dog Jax to the Templeton one this weekend. He had a ball!" A real human adult conversation was happening with my co-worker. I thought to myself, *Wow, how cool am I right now? Oh gosh, I better not act like I think I am cool.* I am just excited to be living my dream and talking to a co-worker in person, like a couple of friends. When we were done, I headed back to the tasting room, knowing I'd definitely missed Josh describe the wines to the customers, but reminded myself there would be plenty of other customers for me to watch him interact with. I walked up the ramp, through the kitchen, and into the tasting room. I joined Josh behind the big oak bar.

I had my notebook with me, and the customers quickly looked at me, then back at Josh and their tasting glasses. Josh leaned over close and said to me, "Just as some may choose to have an espresso after a big meal, a small serving of port can be appropriate in this circumstance" and he offered them one more sample of something not on the limited tasting menu. He said, "I have something special for you guys" as he poured. The customers saw that this pour of liquid was much smaller than the other pours he'd given, he explained about the wine being stronger as it was fortified. I felt their eyes go to me again and I felt on the spot. I grabbed my pen again and wrote down the word fortified with a question mark next to it. I felt I needed to listen better and look up a few things later. He'd moved on to explaining how this is a port wine and it's made in the solera style. I also wrote that down with a question mark behind it, and we made eye contact. He looked at my notes, and he must have noticed I was taking this seriously with my notebook and all. He smiled and continued, "As I am showing my new friend Jenn here, an experienced Sommelier can talk about options for the table's enjoyment and help bringing unity in the bottle selection. For discerning customers, like yourself, an after-meal drink recommendation also provides an extra level of reprieve from having to make yet another decision along with the decision of what to order for dinner. Now, I admit, I am not a Sommelier myself, but I do know these bottles all too well and I can help recommend what else you may like."

They looked at me, and I felt they wanted me to say something, I blurted out, "He certainly seems to know the wine. I trust him already!" I chuckled nervously and they smiled, sniffed and sipped their port wine as I nervously smiled while looking back to my notebook of words to look up later about how to be a wine educator.

When the customers left, their $10 cash tip was revealed sticking half out from under one of their menus. Josh goes to the cash register, breaks the bill into two 5's, hands me one, pockets the other, and turns to me and says, "You should just go ahead and try all the wines now Jenn, because as pourers we have the responsibility to ensure the other guests' experience isn't negatively affected." I am stunned. I earned $5 for standing there listening and now he's offering me drinks. A rush of excitement comes over me, as I could definitely get used to this.

Meeting Josh was the beginning of something. He wasn't cold, like the tasting room's backroom cellar. He was warm and knew how to talk with people. He was certainly fresher than the kitchen where we were to polish wine glasses, and his voice was as soft and sweet as a bottle of Ask Me Nicely wine. His presence reminded me I was a woman. I knew I wasn't only a mother, there to serve others before myself. I was a woman. My sociable extroverted roots were about to get watered. Watered with wine. While my roots felt like they had last been watered a lifetime ago, I was thirsty. Maybe this was where the term, "get your toes wet" comes from, I wondered.

FIRST SIPS

The tasting menu changed from time to time, and it was explained to me that I should try the wine in the order on the sheet of paper, called The Tasting Menu. I should begin with white wine, go to rosé, then end with red, and maybe the port. Josh added, "If you're feeling brave," he said with his crooked smile and tiny chuckle. I worried he'd seen the shyness that I have sometimes, but there was no time for rumination because he continued training me.

Josh continued, "When talking to the people in here, the customer may think they're more of a cabernet person, and don't love merlot, but the best thing they need to pack on their trip here to Paso's wine country, is an open mind. Oh, and an open palate. I hate when they're chewing gum at the bar!" I quickly learned that wine educators have pet peeves about customers, and since they're the ones curating an experience for customers it's best to follow certain best practices of utilizing their knowledge and guidance. Josh teaches me, "When they come to the tasting room with questions and ponderings about wine, the tasting room staff is equipped to answer questions. This is because we have studied wine in college, like Devin, you'll meet him later on, or those who are studying to become a sommelier themselves, like Ambrose. He only works during the week, so sometimes your shifts will align. For all of us though, the time in the tasting room can be an education in and of itself. Also, they may have worked the harvest — they literally had their hand in the wine-making process, from vineyard to bottle, so they see a different angle of it. You'll learn quick here Jenn!"

I tried a sip of the viogner. I think to myself that my three years of high school French classes are coming in handy with the pronunciation of the wine names as I know to pronounce the wine vie-on-yay just as Josh does. I feel like such a poser though, as I've never been to France, and my last passport expired before getting any stamps in it. Plus, I have no idea how he opens the bottle with the corkscrew so fast.

Then, I tried the chardonnay. It's lemony but not sweet like lemonade, and I'm reminded of my kitchen sink cleaner. The aroma of lemon without the tartness. I read the tasting notes on the menu and it reads, "This chardonnay opens on the nose with Meyer lemon rind, green apple, toasty oak, and lychee. A taste reveals notes of creamy lemon bar and tropical fruit. The wine finishes with crème brûlée and biscuit." I inwardly smile thinking I, too, like to finish my meal with a crème brûlée for dessert. Overall, all I know is that I like the fresh flavor and feel like this is some basic type of wine my mom would probably like.

Next, I try the rosé. Thankful to French class once again, I know to say rose-ayy and not simply rose like the flower. The bottle is clear and has a fish on its label, and I wonder if this implies it has notes of seafood or if it pairs with fish. I look, and the tasting notes on the menu say, "Drinkability meets complexity in a refreshing, bone-dry pink that will charm its way onto any patio. This lively rosé shows an enticing mix of orange and pink colors that brighten with time. On the nose there's rich raspberry, strawberry, and zesty citrus. The palate is dry, with thrist-quenching acidity and a smooth fruit finish." I'm excited for this as that description sounds like something Anthony Bourdain would say, and I love him. I asked Josh what it means to be "bone-dry" as bones seem inherently wet as they're in our bodies and covered by blood and guts and such. Josh teaches me that it just means it's not sweet, and to remember it like humor…clarifying that dry humor isn't sweet, but it can still be great. I feel that that's my first wine mnemonic of sorts, and I appreciate the connection. I still don't understand the watercolor painted fish reference, but I sure am feeling like a fish out of water. Starting with how I even held the glass wrong, and fretted about saying the wrong thing. I finally take a sip of the rosé, and it's delicious and I understand what they mean about the patio, as I would love to drink this at one of my book club meetings if we were all gathering outside.

He apparently thinks my drink needs a drink because before I am even done swallowing the last bit of the rosé, he pours a little red wine in my glass and tells me I should try this zinfandel blend. It's special because we can grow it here as it's hot enough to ripen the fruits. He adds that it's juicy, and not too dry. He pauses, and smiles when he says, "It's called Maelstrom… because it just swirls down your throat, meaning it's easy to drink."

I ponder his description, the tasting notes, and the menu sheet that reads, "Seductive notes of sweet tobacco and pine that welcome you into a glass that's heavy with dark fruit notes of blackberry, black cherry and plum. After the word "seductive" the second thing I notice are the words, "92 pts Wine Enthusiast" and begin by asking him what that means. Josh explains that Wine Enthusiast magazine had a wine competition and it was scored 92 out of 100, "but that doesn't really mean anything to how good it is, just to how good it was to a certain judge on a certain day." He adds that he doesn't use those ratings when drinking wine, but mentions that some people do. And remembers that sometimes people even come here just for that reason. I was surprised to hear people travel for wine, and that there are wine competitions, and even a magazine all about wine. I was so happy to be learning about this whole wine world that exists so outside of my realm and glad to be in good hands with Josh training me.

I try another zinfandel blend. This one is dark and looks smaller in my glass. I learn to swirl the wine in the glass like Josh does — to hold the stick part of the glass, which is called the stem, and circle the base of the glass ever so gently on the bar, just a slight movement but enough to make the wine swirl and twirl in the glass. He told me this wine's grapes grow across the street from the other, and I imaged cars and trucks rushing by spewing exhaust on the vines as they honk on by. But it's not like that at all. It's part of a huge vineyard full of acres and acres of vines, so the cars really have no effect on the wine. This particular wine blend is called Preciosa , and scored lower, at 90 points from Wine Enthusiast magazine. Despite that, its description is enticing to me. It reads, "This zinfandel has a strong aroma of vanilla, roasted nuts, and candied apple. The palate is thick with notes of raspberry, rhubarb, red apple, coconut, bay leaf with a lingering pepper finish."

I put together what I observed, and swirled, then lifted it by the stem, and bring the glass to my nose. I inhale, take it in, and smell it, and then take a little sip to taste it. Then, slowly placed the glass back down, and swirled again, and pondered the juice's flavor.

Josh says, "This one's a bit of a late bloomer." Oh, he's going to sound like the great foodie and cultural anthropologist Anthony Bourdain too? I thought, and my expression must have read as "go on" because he continued, "It's because of its location in the vineyard. The wine's flavor is changed as the grapes ripen slowest. Something to do with the sunshine and shade."

This wine, or maybe the fact that it's my fifth, or sixth, tasting in a row, is speaking to me. I feel a connection with this wine's description, and I feel like such a late bloomer too. In my mid-thirties and just now learning how to swirl, sip, and savor. I can hardly describe the things I'm noticing in the wine, will that skill bloom next? I certainly hope so, but as of right now, I also feel like a young school girl in utter awe at this young man who is describing grape juice so eloquently to me.

"Now, let's have you try our Bordeaux blend. We call it Aeon. It's Latin for *ages*. You probably think that's cute huh?" Josh asked. I ask, "So people drink this on their anniversary, or Valentine's Day?" grasping at straws as what to ask about the wine. I see on the tasting menu, it's described as "elegant Bordeaux blend begins with aromas of mint, rhubarb, blueberry, and dark fruit on the nose. Soft and pretty hint of sweet oak and clove combine on the palate to make the bright tannins in this wine shine through." I think with that description of such drink-able sexiness and a $44 price tag, I know this is bound to be deli-cious. Josh pours me a little bit, I estimate two ounces, and remind myself to smell it before sipping, so I gently grab my glass in the way Josh always does, by the stem, under the goblet part, and slowly bring it to my lips. Tilting the glass to my nose, I inhale and smell dark fruit as described, but struggle to notice the mint or rhubarb. I thought to myself, "rhubarb, isn't that the red celery thing they turn into pies, right" I maaaybe smell rhubarb pie, but I'm lying to myself with the power of sugges-tion, as I've never ordered rhubarb pie in my entire life as the much more delicious fruit, strawberries, exist. I set the glass down and smile.

"Remember that port wine we talked about? You won't be able to go back and drink another red wine after this one, as it has been known to mess with your taste buds. It's strong!" he emphasized with raised eyebrows.

Josh explained that I may be surprised how much this region and winemaker's expertise can affect someone's preferences. They may walk away with a new favorite. He tells me, they are coming to us to explain the wine's content, origin, and food pair-ings. "This will help you if you know this...you need to under-stand its place and how to best enjoy it."

"Its place?" I wonder, and understand that this place is certainly a world in itself, so of course it has its own rules and vocabulary.

"Trust us that a lot of thought and expertise went into the wine flight list and especially to its order — its place on the lineup. Sometimes people embarrass themselves and don't want to stick to following the flow for the best tasting experience. I also hate it when they don't savor their sips. They're over here guzzling it down at 10 in the morning! I don't expect them to remember the exact nuances of the bottle's flavor profile, but you're here already people, allow yourself the pleasure of noticing the feeling of whether you liked it or not."

WHERE WE'RE AT

The city's full name is El Paso De Robles, meaning The Pass of the Oaks. However, locals call is Paso (pronounced Pass-OH!). It has often been called the "new Napa" but it really doesn't need to be a "new" anything because it's enough of a place to stand on its own. While the Paso Robles wine region shares the state with Napa and is approximately 250 miles south in San Luis Obispo County, it is a world apart. With Paso being equidistant from San Francisco and Los Angeles, the area embodies half and half Gemini qualities. It's hot in the summer and cold in the winter. It's cowboy, but it's also fancy, and at times flip floppy as there's a big water park on the east side of town. The area has copious vineyards, picturesque views, and hundreds of winery tasting rooms. Within the area of Paso Robles, there's variations in the elevations, proximity to the ocean, and areas that have different weather and thus, different vine growing areas of specialty. Just like people, there's different sides to Paso.

We have these areas called microclimates, which are areas of different weather, throughout the county. What these microclimates have that makes Paso special, is the ability to produce different variances in the grapes and even within that grape varietal, based on their growing conditions. For example, I learned that a zinfandel growing on Paso's Westside varies from a zinfandel grown on Paso's Eastside. Highway 101 serves as the delineator between East and West. There are professionals that organize such geekery and have categorized the Paso Robles region into 11 American Viticulture Areas. These are called AVA's, for short, and are a designated wine grape growing regions. This means within the Paso area there's 11 specific regions present. These regions are appellations that grow different vines and these opportunities allow the wine taster to see how distinct areas effect wine. Terroir, pronounced "tear-hua," is another element that adds to the complexity of these regions. It looks awfully close to the word "terrior" which is a kind of short-statured and often shaggy dog, so please take note of the OI not the IO spelling in the word. Terroir can influence a grape varietal, in that the density of difference in the sunshine and soil can produce very different results. Add in a whole lotta love and the region's vines can yield enough juice to make a dehydrated Bacchus happy.

In these rolling hills and bucolic roadways, winery tasting rooms are sometimes close together, uniting in the proximity, and elsewise their ruralness has them standing apart up on a hill. Sometimes the vines you see growing on the hills are next to their tasting room and their in-house enologist also known as the scientist behind the wine, and winemaker, use what's growing outside their door to make the wine. Also, sometimes the juice from the grape's harvest is sold to winemakers who do not tend to the land themselves and focus on the making, storage or distribution processes. Some do both.

HOSPITALITY

A constant learner, I was first to sign up for the Hospitality Training session that was advertised on our kitchen fridge which was essentially our break room. The manager at the time, Tammy, joined me, and we attended together. The training was put on by Forbes Travel Guide and was designed to enhance staff skills and inspire us to deliver exceptional guests experiences. There were about 50 of us in the training. In a get-to-know-you part of the session, I met many other people who worked at wineries in the area but the most important man was our teacher for the day, Pablo Duran. The class was an all-day event in the banquet room at a local hotel which is about a mile and a half from the tasting room. We were taught a lot! Customer Service, Hospitality, and the Service Sector sometimes get a bad rap when people leave reviews on Yelp and Google Reviews, but he really made me believe there should be some respect for the people whose profession requires them to refrain from saying 85% of the things they wish they could say in public.

Pablo told us that having customers from all over the world came with a big responsibility, as it heightened the expectations put on us from this global platform. It was true that Paso is getting more and more popular, and that people were coming from all over the world to this region, but I hadn't thought of it as a responsibility before. He explained further saying that, "More people expect world class service and it's our job to elevate the luxury in the service world."

This line of work was like Adulting, but on the global stage.

This traditionally is not a profession people dream about doing. They did not make a "When I grow up…" posterboards or essays and talk about crafting experiences for others on vacation. It's only for the type of people-pleasers who love making people happy who come to, and stay in, this profession. Basically, it's the people who want to create meaning and purpose for their people-pleasing nature. Pablo motivated us to learn his tricks as he told us that the hospitality industry is the only industry in which you could decide how much money you take home. He said this is because if you go above and beyond what was expected you can make an emotional connection and that's where you get tipped. We were asked to come up with things we could do for our guests, and contribute ideas to the group. One woman said, "If he likes football, I can introduce him to my neighbor's cousin's brother who knows that football player Jason Kelce."

Pablo smiled, and replied, "Yes if that's true, and you can really make that happen. Anyone else want to share your ideas?" "We could write Happy Birthday on a wine bottle, if it was their birthday," someone in the back of the room contributed. "I could call a restaurant and get them dinner reservations," someone at the side of the room contributes. "I also could call my friend who works at another tasting room and make them a reservation for their next stop on their wine tasting day," someone in front me said. I decided to share an idea I had done before when I made the customers happy. I raised my hand, and began to speak, "I could giftwrap the bottle, if it was a present for their house sitter, mailman, or AirBnB hosts or whomever." When I spoke up, I heard my voice rattle. This was a good, solid, and very doable idea. It was a very *me* idea. I don't know why I was shy about my contribution. I had been a house sitter before and would have been thrilled being gifted a bottle of wine, and wouldn't have really cared if it was gift wrapped or not. Generally, I really do appreciate presentation when giving gifts. Heck, I even loved presentation when seeing others give gifts. I think it really adds something in the suspense and surprise of the experience. One of my Love Languages is gifts, so I should have been more confident in my contribution to the classroom discussion. I reflected afterwards and noticed that I am better in smaller groups of people, than large groups like this. But I wanted to show my boss Tammy that I have ideas too, and that I wasn't taking a backseat to this training course.

Pablo seemed pleased with my idea. He replied, saying "Yes! That's a good one," in the way teachers do. He encouraged these ideas, and told us what's important is to make an emotional connection, he suggested we craft incredibly unique experiences and exclusive access and add a line in the interaction, like, "This is not something we typically do" and yes, it may take more effort from us, but that's exactly what guests want to see us do — sweat for them. Well kind of sweat, more like they want to experience us making an exception for them.

Pablo said that this was how we could create a guest for life before frequently used amenities lose value. Meaning that if we give the world to everyone, the world was less meaningful. He said, "We need to be nimble which lets us create tailored experiences for guest after guest." This meant we needed to adjust our script, our repertoire as people's desires on vacation, and in winery establishments change from their normal lives. Basically, we were responsible for sweating the details so they (the customer) didn't have to. Pablo made us all chuckle when he told us, "The customer only has to show up…and pay!"

The session concluded with the knowledge that once we begin this type of service, it would just get easier for us, as making people happy was addictive. We also would see commerce in a different way. I now know there's more to people's work smiles. That the kindness from someone like the barista at Starbucks wasn't necessarily due to their genuine kindness but may be fueled by their hope for a tip. Or maybe when you work for a larger business than Stonefruit Canyon, this type of knowledge was part of their employee handbook and onboarding training process. The dopamine rush of a job well done feels so rewarding to our people-pleasing nature it's great to know exactly how to do it. This was the kind of knowledge that makes people like me stay in the customer service industry as it fulfills a deep desire to make the world a better place.

I liked how Pablo began the day with the promise of money and finished it with some heart. He definitely knew how to talk to us and motivate us to create curated experiences that would feel exclusive in the efforts to get tips, create lifelong customers, and fuel our addiction of making people happy. What I took from that day stuck with me for a long time. The job was more meaningful than simple customer service. It was offering customers the quiet luxury of being cared for, and cared about.

MEOW TO LOVE

I had more coworkers to meet, and learned there was even two of them with four feet, erm, paws. The cats of Stonefruit Canyon included Georgia, a Maine Coon cat and Sophia, a Siamese mix. I was mostly a dog person up until working at Stonefruit Canyon. Previously, the closest I came to being a cat lady was when I practiced cat pose in yoga, but was easily charmed by these two felines. I considered them my co-workers too and set out to learn all about them. I was curious. I studied their behavior, likes and dislikes, and noticed how customers even came in asking for them, proving I wasn't the only one taken by their majestic nature. Georgia was more interactive with me at first. She seemed to take joy keeping me busy by letting her in and out of the tasting room doors. She would look through the glass panes of the French doors and stare at me longing to come inside. Then, once inside, she would do a loop to check out the tasting room, then returned to the window and stare out at nature, longing to get back out there. Cats struggle with making up their mind about us humans, I learned. What she did love most of all was to explore the expansive property, on her terms though. She must have had the property lines measured as she never strayed too far. She also loved being perched on the rooftop by the entrance of the tasting room. Like I learned cats do, she liked to judge us humans. I liked to tease that she's the official winery greeter. She would stare everyone down as they walked from their car, ride shares, or even bicycles all the way through to the winery's welcome sign. To receive thanks for this service, she was paid in various Meow Mix and Greenies treats. She had a fluffy bed in the cellar and is officially fed two times a day in there, although she took her organic snacks into her own hands and hunts field mice in the vineyard. She should have been reimbursed for this service too, come to think of it. Pest control is a big deal in rural communities, like the outskirts of Paso. She was endearing, and thanks to a quick google, she was like all Maine Coon mixes, and had mega floofy fur. What surprised me most about her, was her habit of drool. I never knew a cat to do that! She was known to drool when held for a long time, and it's the closest she ever came to being a dog, not that I would ever compare her to one in her company. Cats hate that. Georgia was loved by many who come to visit, try wine, and check in on her. Some came for her first and the wine, second.

The Cat Distribution System, the unofficial way of the world in which people obtain cats, gave Stonefruit Canyon a second feline friend. This second cat was named Sophia. I was told she's a blend of Siamese and Russian Blue. She was daintier footed that Georgia, and has decided to do what she wants in her age of wisdom. Older than Georgia, but a tight-lipped lady who never reveals her age, she is a bit shy and spends more time behind the scenes of the tasting room. She preferred being in the office section of the building, than the busy bar space. I was told by Tom that she is mostly blind, but if you notice her behavior like I have long enough, you see the truth. She most definitely can see, and I sense she was labeled "blind" by a person *ahem* Tom *ahem* who loves dogs more. I was once like Tom too, but these cats were so fun to observe and wonder about. I liked the slow burn nature of their love. I really had to work for their attention sometimes, and they made me feel like I was a guest that ought to behave in their home. I obliged. Sophia had a rough time living in the tasting room. She was startled by loud noise, particularly those humans who get louder as they drink alcohol. While she did adapt and learn to avoid them, we all try to be a little quieter when she's around; I know I do, at least. Sophia also avoids workers carrying 55-pound cases of wine. That's when I discovered she most definitely can see! She's observant in that way, knowing that when us workers carry big boxes, she could get underfoot easier. This small behavior of hers proves to me she has all her five senses at work for her. Like Georgia, she is also fed in the cellar and has a cozy slate grey colored cat bed there too. When it's tasting room closing time, she is housed in the cellar overnight for safety. Unlike Georgia who roams free at night, Sophia does not hunt for rodent snacks like Georgia, so she gets to receive more of her snacks picked out for her. Sophia routinely enjoys her little green, fish-shaped cat treats, that are placed on her bed for her to enjoy before bedtime.

Being motherly in nature, I got Sophia in the cellar at closing time by calling out, "Come on Sophia, it's tuck tuck time!" This is a call paying homage to how I and my son referred to bedtime as "tuck tuck time." These cats are my at-work children. When I call that out, Sophia, as if on cue, would follow me into the cellar. It felt so dang good being able to observe and love on Georgia and Sophia in the tasting room. Don't tell my dog Luna, but I admit, there had been a change in me. I had changed in the most unexpected of ways — I had quickly become a very odd thing. A Cat Person.

BETTY

Betty was hired shortly after I was, so I got to be there for her interview. Well, not in the room-there, but in the building when she came out and told us she got the job and would see us next week. When next week came, she was noticeably dressed up. Still in the mood to observe fashion, our uniform consisted of any t-shirt with the words Stonefruit Canyon on it, and pants of our choosing. Most of us wore jeans, slacks or khakis. But today, Betty's first day, Betty already broke this rule by wearing black polyester dressy pants with a big silver buckle and a light asymmetrical cut sweater. She was professionally trendy. Her thick black hair was long and she was generously tattooed. In addition to the visible ones, in parts of the sweater's lacier parts, like on her elbows and shoulder areas, even more of her tattoos could be seen. She wore leopard-print flats and was, what I estimated, five foot 10 inches tall. All that to say, when she walked into a room, like this tasting room, her presence was noticed. She spoke a tad louder than I usually do, as often my nervous voice trembles or stutters when I speak. Betty was a mega babe, and walked with a confidence as she took up space physically and with her voice. Mega babe for sure, as far as I could see! I wanted to be like her in many ways, so I paid close attention and set a personal goal to get to know her.

She made this easy for me, in that she was happy to talk about herself. I wanted to know about her family, and how she, as a single mother, was able to work full-time. I found it incredibly challenging to even fit part-time work into my life, and she was doing it full-time. Incredible. She shared about all the family she has in the area, and how she "hardly ever leaves Templeton, but sometimes goes to Paso." She added that she was going through a divorce, and before that ran a tattoo shop with her husband. Ah, the ink coverage was making sense now — it was a family tradition! My family didn't make a tradition of fashion like that, but we all seemed to appreciate style in the form of Norm Core, if maybe slightly 90's preppy and basic colors and traditional pairings that can be called anything but hashtaggable. Betty was cool, I could tell right away.

When Tom made an appearance in the tasting room, our conversations stopped. He asked Betty for her documents for the new hire paperwork and then stopped in his tracks when he noticed her outfit. Eyeing her up and down, he apologized that he didn't offer her one free Stonefruit Canyon t-shirt already. She leaned her elbow on the bar and said, "I'm sorry, but I am uncomfortable dressing down in this environment." Tom did that eye squinty thing I had seen in my interview and that I now recognized as a sign of his anxiety, and after 30 seconds that felt like the whole of eternity replied with, "let's talk outside." They walked down the steps to the backyard area behind the tasting room and in the middle of the yard space, he sat at one of the dozen or so white picnic benches. He sat on the bench, and she on the table — a Queen! Towering over him I would have given my left eye to hear what they were talking about.

Betty is full of sass and commands full respect at the same time. Not only is she artistically tattooed, she has an edge that made her get promoted quickly where she proved to be an incredible manager. I imagined that her no-nonsense way helped her when she was going through a divorce, too. Looking at her, she really is a Betty. She's an uncanny combination of Betty Boop and Bettie Page. Despite this femme fetal nature of her, she's also a tad shy and keenly observant. She's a serial dater and drives an X-series BMW. While she is too timid to drive the 101, she isn't too timid when setting the rules for the tasting room. She stood up to the boss about the casual uniforms and noticed that the sunshine in the tasting room window, making the clothes get faded where the sun shone. The clothes have been there a while and were fading faster than the crowd of a Rebelution or Snoop Dog concert. Betty really had a beef with the t-shirts there. They came in very limited sizes and didn't accommodate those who had nothing better in their life to do that work out. Both Betty and I were midsize with a little extra Venusian curves and needed to wear the men's sizing to make it fit. I played along, but Betty refused the outfit all together. She spoke with the manager and negotiated that as long as she was dressed classy and could perform her job's duties, she would be choosing her own outfits. Single handedly, she forever changed the tasting room rules. This was the first lesson I learned from her — you can be casual or more formal, as long as it matched the environment you were in, but most importantly, it needed to match who you are on the inside.

On our bar, the dump buckets, which are formally called spittoons, are for gently and subtlety dumping, aka, pouring wine into. Customers do this for many reasons such as not wanting to drink all the wine offered in tastings to preserve their palate, and to stay sober. We were trained that the bucket is emptied out into another bucket at the end of the shift as part of closing procedures. Nicole asked why we don't just make it simple and pour it down the sink, to which we were told that too much alcohol was bad for the plumbing. Tom said, "I have had many a customer offer to take the bucket home, quoting that "alcohol kills germs," and we saw his inner germaphobe shudder at the thought.

One morning before any customers came, Betty and I were chitchatting getting to know each other and she asked me, "Jenn, who is your celebrity crush?" I thought about it for a moment, and replied, "Santa Claus." I could tell by the look in her eyes that wasn't the answer she expected. I really wanted hurry up and elaborate that it was their Hygge-like cozy nature and generous happiness and masculinity that was endearing to me. She told Josh when he came into the tasting room, "Josh, get a load of this! Jenn likes when Santa sips wine and his beard brushes the wine in his glass. O.M.G...her new nickname has got to be 'Christmas!'" Josh smiled at me and said, "Christmas it is then." And I felt some relief that he would assume my type would only be Santas, and that would deter him from ever noticing it was he whom I also had a crush on. Between Betty teasing me and giving me a nickname, it showed she really thought about what I said. I felt she had indulged my wild idea, taking it even further with the detail about his beard getting wine on it when he sipped, and knew me just barely enough to tease me about it. To me, that's the moment when the work cama- raderie between us began to feel like friendship.

A DAY IN THE LIFE

W hen I drove into work and I would notice how the hills around the tasting room looked like a Microsoft screen saver. It's idyllic and the rains have watered the grass so they're bright green and full of health. The crisp Kelly-green rolling hills have even shades of green represented when you really look at it. The blades of grass remind me of various crayons in the big 96 Crayola crayon box with the sharpener on the back. Crayola gave us just enough colors to make up this landscape. I noticed how the grapes look like speckles of green and then morphed to purple through their life cycle. I noticed the various orange and blue wildflowers which grew on the ground between the seemingly endless rows of vines.

Working in the opening shift gave me some slow time in the tasting room and allowed me to slow down and learn the behind the scenes setting up the tasting rooms. I really cared about this job and the environment. It seemed that there were folks just passing through this place, too. Like how we would tune radio stations in the 90's. Turning the dial from one station to another, and turning away when it played too much static.

While this was the setting for poetry, I had practical things to do and didn't dwell on the beauty too much. I had to open the curtains, wiping down the tables outside. I had to look at the wine in the back stock and make sure one of each bottle that is on the tasting menu is open and in line. This essentially is what the French call, *mise en platz* and is a preparation of materials needed. For me this meant to set up the bar side that I'll be working at and making sure we have wine and polished glasses. This is also making sure that the bottles that are hidden behind the bar for quick sale are well stocked. This is looking if there's any reservations for the day and putting up a reserved sign on the table. This is knowing what party sizes are happening and what tables need to be set up to accommodate them comfortably. This is also knowing what events are happening in the area. For if there's a car showing in Morro Bay or an art lavender festival in Paso, those might bring extra crowds. Knowing what times are these things over is the important part, because that's undoubtedly when we will have the crowd of people rushing in.

There were some tricks we did when it was mere ten minutes to closing time and we couldn't give another customer a full experience tasting in that time. We would tilt the blinds ever so slightly in efforts to look more closed than we were. This helped prevent a last-minute group from coming in for what they call a "quick taste." Josh told me in the training that, "People that always want a 'quick taste' are never the quickest drinkers! They're always, well truly nearly always, the slowest drinkers and they hardly ever buy after having a sample. I avoid them at all costs." Noted.

I prepped for the day by fluffing the pillows and making sure there's not some lizard or mouse that Georgia has half eaten lying lifeless in the walkway. This meant walking the perimeter of the backyard and making sure there's no gravel, rocks or twigs and branches in the way. Sometimes there's disgusting elements too. Gross like a trashcan that didn't get taken out the night before by the closing crew and by the mornings' sunshine, it likely has attracted a copious number of flies or ants. So, I will take care of what needs to be taken care of in efforts to make a magical little backyard for our future guests to enjoy. Contriving nature like this feels Disneylandish. Like I am manicuring the environment to suit our vibe, but it's part of the preparations to begin the day for me as well. It's my routine, my *mise en platz*, if you will.

THE HAPPINESS OF HENRY

As part of my training, I met and worked with Henry. It was a Friday and I was told Henry is part time too but I would always work with him on Fridays. This job attracted such different types of people that I met so far. I was curious who I'd meet next.

I saw him from across the tasting room. He was on the far-left side of the bar, by the adjacent fireplace. He was talking to a customer and pouring them a red wine when I approached. Henry taught me about himself before we even got to the wine, or tasting room rules. That's because his outfit and general persona spoke pretty loudly. I could tell right away that he was the type of guy who was authentically himself. I thought he also played the Old Man Card a lot, and would ask for a Senior Discount at diners. He wasn't the type to put up with bullshit, nor be the bullshit.

When Henry has a pause in his description about the wine, Josh interjects and tells Henry that I'm training to be a wine educator. At that exact moment Henry is distracted by a kiddo chasing Georgia, and he looked up and over at me. He makes a "tisk" sound and in the middle of the cat and kid wrangling, advises me, "Do a little research if you plan to bring a large party to the winery...by large I mean being a party over 4 guests. Like these people, coming in with grandma and aunts, uncles and such. The whole gang. Luckily, I kind of could help them, but if this was on a Saturday, we couldn't. So, tell people to avoid getting turned away for having too large of a party in too small of a tasting room. I'm not a bad guy, generally, I like children, and well-behaved children are always welcome, but to avoid a small tasting room from being overwhelmed it's better to make sure there's an outside area to comfort, or distract a child, if the need arises." The man could talk. He was talking to me, I was sure of it by the eye contact, but he was actually discretely talking to the customers and reprimanding them about their ill-behaved children. He definitely didn't give any more than one, single solitary shit.

Eloquence while frustrated was one of Henry's many skills. Also, internalizing the stories of the wine, coincides with the internalizing the wine itself. This is something Henry excelled at. When talking to the customers he would tell the most magical story of the location of the grapes, the science behind the winery, and the happenstance of the grapes growing that particular year. He talked to customers in a way that showed the story of the grape's journey. Working with him was like hanging out with a fun grandpa. Not a grandfather but a grandpa like the cool, easy-going version of the elder family member. He was more on our side than the side of the parents, ahem boss. Henry would be casual about imparting his wisdom to us working in the tasting room. He reserved his knowledge for the right moment, and was patient enough to wait for the perfect time to tell a joke, too. He understood that the guests want to have a story to tell their friends. He did this by being memorable.

Henry understood that this job was a casual fun part-time job that was meant to be enjoyed. His slappy demeanor also came across as confidence, but with a hint of reserve from him too, as he didn't talk as much as Josh did. It's as if Henry knew he was only getting paid a tad over minimum wage, and it was okay as it was his 'stepping out of retirement job' but darn it, he was going to have fun at it. Well, as much fun as someone not in full retire-ment could have. This seemed like a nice balance for Henry. He could get people slightly tipsy drunk while taking sips of his own between pouring for others. He got a little extra spending money, and an industry discount at other wineries. Henry's wisdom and knowledge about wine was put on the backburner when he asked some customers how they like the wine. He followed up with this sage advice, "Wine doesn't always need to be understood to be enjoyed. Taste it. Savor the flavor. The only thing to ask yourself in this moment is, 'Do I like it?'" as he smiles a charmingly confident smile as if he's just hacked the entire purpose in life.

Looking deeper at Henry, I observed a lot during our shifts together. I learned he's in his mid-60's, a former professor at USC, frazzle-haired, and scrappy. Despite this outward appearance, he's authored three books. We affectionately nicknamed him our Grandpa Henry as he was always giving wine knowledge and life advice to the younger staff. On his days off he spent time building a water fountain at his house as a memorial to his late father. He's sentimental. He describes Malbec as "luscious" and says it in a way that definitely lets you know this wine is his favorite. I started copying this too, and can't say the word *luscious* without thinking of Henry. It's a fun word to say, when you think about it. It feels good in your mouth. *Luscious.* It makes you smile when saying it.

HE SAID WHAT?

G etting more comfortable at my job, I learned that working with the general public is very different than helping online students one-on-one as their tutor. First of all, the general public is much more, stranger-centric, which means I don't know these people whatsoever, but I have to be very nice to them. And in return, the strangers would say and do anything to me. But then in turn, I'd be so nice to them. It's really a very unique work environment. I imagined if I had gotten that beer bar job, what would have happened to me. I had weird things happen at Stone-fruit Cellars as it was. One time someone told me, "You look like a very, very old Arya Stark in Game of Thrones." On my break, I Googled her. She was gorgeous, and having a slight resemblance to her was a compliment. But I remember then saying "very" two times before "old" which forced me to feel like crap. My age played no factor in my being able to do my job well. I wondered why they would judge me for that, and if I should've said something back to them. At the time, I had no retort, but the comment likely would keep me awake that night. Josh must have sensed my reaction to this customer's comment and knew I didn't watch the show, so he graciously took the conversation to this week's episode instead and rambled on with the customers. While it was usually pretty strict in the tasting room about "these are my customers, so I earn their tip" there were moments when we came to each other's rescue out of sheer cringe at the situation we were each in. Someone on the outside could swoop in and handle it with fresh eyes. I was so thankful for Josh in this moment. He didn't even have to hear me share I was confused and upset, he just knew. It amazed me that a guy could ever read my mind. That was a new one for me!

Another memorable time when pouring wine in a customer's glass, the customer forcefully grabbed my elbow and lifted it in the air, which tilted the bottle and made more wine to pour in their glass. I was shocked that he touched me, but thought quick and responded by saying, "you can trust me to give you a nice heavy pour. We don't have serving regulators on our bottles here at Stonefruit Canyon." However eloquent I was under pressure, like Betty, Henry, and Josh taught me to be, I couldn't quite conjure a toothy smile after that one. A simple customer service smile is all I could muster.

Thankfully it was almost time for my ten-minute break. During my break, I walked to my car and sat in the passenger's seat. I breathed deeply and remembered what my mom would tell me when I would get upset. "Jenn, use your yoga breathing, and remember it will be okay," she'd say. Yoga had been in my life since I was ten years old and she signed me up for a class through our city's recreation department. I still even practiced from time to time. I knew the things I had been taught were so helpful in calming my anxious mind, and helping me connect my brain back to my body. So, I sat there and practiced my deep breaths, which yogis called Ujjayi Breathing. I did a handful of breath cycles. Afterwards, I did feel calmer, and my rushing blood didn't feel so loud in my veins. I opened my eyes and surveyed my environment. It was warm and being on Paso's westside, the tasting room parking lot had some wind paired alongside the heat. I saw the oak trees' leaves sway. As the sun shown down, and the warmth touched my skin, it was the perfect setting to calm myself in. It was beautiful, but I rolled up my window and I turned on my car to center myself even better in the air conditioning. It was a short break, but the time felt so precious to me that it was worth turning my car on and using up a little gas, for the mere seven more minutes left over on my break. I closed my eyes and focused on my breath as I felt how the cool wind on my face sort of numbed my skin.

My alarm rang, signaling that my break was over. I was too tired these days to trust myself to not nod off while meditating, so I set an alarm. I turned off my car and walked back inside the tasting room. I saw Henry who was carrying wine bottles out to the same customers I tended to inside. I recognized the man who grabbed my arm. He was on the edge of the group. As Henry was heading to that entire group who was sitting outside, I grabbed the door for him. There were six white picnic tables in the backyard of the tasting room. Three had umbrellas and the others let the sun shine on the customer. He approached the group who chose the table with an umbrella. This made sense as it was hot out and Henry already had a hint of sweat on his brow and darkening grey areas of cotton in his armpits showing he had been sweating. In this moment Henry was very self-aware. As he served them the wine, he must have noticed how the heat was getting to him, and he smiled while he looked at me and then back to the customers and said, "Sunlight is a good thing actually. As Galileo Galilei said, 'Wine is sunlight held together by water.' This is pretty special because we're made up of water too. So if you think about it, we're pretty close to being wine ourselves."

The joke fell flat. No giggle or not even a couple nods. I was cleaning off a table nearby, and when I heard Henry using his famous Galileo quote on customers and I expected it would usually get him a few laughs. This table was full of people who comedians call a tough crowd. They were rude to me inside the tasting room, and didn't understand Henry's humor either. However, there was more to this story in store for me, because just then, the customer leaned over on the bench, as if to talk to just me and loudly said, "Oh, did he mean the astrology guy Galileo, because I'm a Taurus." I stopped as I was cleaning up from customers at a nearby table, and chuckled; noticing that he mixed up astrology and astronomy. I placated him and got him back for being rude inside, by replying, "Haha, just like the car!" as I walked away.

ALOHA

"Wine is not just an object of pleasure, but an object of knowledge; and the pleasure depends on the knowledge."
Roger Scruton

Devin, my youngest coworker, was pouring for a couple wearing matching Hawaiian shirts when I came into work to do my shift. I could tell he was a bit over their presence as he was standing away from them and leaning at the back bar area. They were doing that cute thing couples do on vacation some- times — matching. They matched each other and their activity for the day. He was doing that very Devin thing where he answered their questions in such a way as to be pompous and knowledgeable, but I could tell he was also tired. Perhaps he stayed up too late the night before, studying, or partying, I thought. Wanting to help my coworker out and actually feeling prepared to do so, I noticed the work of replenishing the bar area of bottles we already sold in the day would be a good use of my time, so I started chatting the couple up.

"I love your shirts where did you get them?" I asked, in effort to make conversation and be a 'master of small talk' that Josh said we ought to be.

"An Etsy shop online!" the woman of the duo replied with so much enthusiasm I thought she may have made the iron-on decal with a Cricut brand crafting machine herself. I wanted to get them chatting and relaxing a bit so I asked them how they're enjoying the wine bottles that Devin had poured already, and which wineries they picked out to try today. The female answered again and told me about visiting Paso's square downtown and Atascadero's downtown as well, and hope to have dinner at that quirky little cash-only steakhouse in Santa Margarita. They said they loved wine, but at the same time as they didn't want to over-do themselves. I admire their knowledge about pacing themselves, as I do the same thing even though I have access to some of the best wines in the world nearby.

"Well, it's a great place for a vacation" I said. The man now told me that he hardly likes wine, and is more of a spirit-sipping kind of guy. He said he loves Mai Tai's and that's why they wore these brightly colored shirts today. "Hawaiian print to represent where I like to drink, and wine glasses and vines to represent what she likes to drink."

I notice now how her shirt was in fact very California Wine Country themed versus traditional his Hawaiian themed with hibiscus and surf waves across the chest of the shirt. "Pretty unique design, for sure. I love Etsy for custom and unique things like that. That's great you two are doing something you both like." And I look at Devin, who is feet away from us now, noticing I have his customers handled. The small talk must have been getting to him, as I correctly guessed. I came up with some excuse about him checking on the refilling the paper towels in the bathrooms as the bulk order had just come in, which gave him the perfect excuse to leave the bar area and head to the back room. Devin understood the assignment and seemed relieved to leave the bar. I was able to help him and utilize the unwritten rule about who pours the wine for who at the tasting room. Generally, the rule states that men pour for women, and women pour for men. Henry and I poured for older patrons and those exploring Paso for their vacation, and Betty poured for people who arrived on motorcycle and those with tattoos. Ambrose and

Josh would pour for groups of young women, namely Bache-lorette parties, and we could all join efforts if the group was big and of mixed types of people. Devin would pour for people who seems to like the technical aspect of things. This was kind of archaic and stereotypical, looking back, but it was for ease of communication and to make a faster connection. We also did this for more tips, of course. We didn't even really address this prac-tice other than what I noticed when someone would say, "these look like your kind of people, Jenn." Or when others would hear the rumble of a motorcycle outside and say, "Betty, I hear your customers coming!" on the times there was two of us up next and due to pour wine for the next customers. Elsewise, we tried to be very fair and give people equal number of groups to pour for. I knew this was conducted in similar style of who gets to wait on particular tables at restaurants. We all want it fair so one worker isn't overwhelmed with customers while another wine educator is polishing glasses for far too much of the majority of their shift. These inner workings were always hidden to me as a customer, and I love that I get to know them now.

SNAPSHOTS

Our new coworker Riley was truly a Jill-of-All-Trades. She told us how she was a former EMT Medic and would be able to tell if people were too drunk to serve. After work she was a photographer, and she scrolled through a few photos on her phone, I could tell she very talented. When she ordered her lunch for pickup from the nearby Mexican restaurant, I learned she was fluent in Spanish. She told us she loved to travel the world, and that's how she met the love of her life in Belize. She shared a picture of the two of them together, and explained how she was still back in Belize and how they were fighting immigration tooth and nail to bring her to the United States. I imagined having a love so strong it could span thousands of miles. The winery wanted to embrace social media, and had us workers take photographs for the marketing campaigns they were setting up. Riley was uber helpful on photographing things. There was a time we had to come to work on a slow day to help stage bottles in gift packaging. I was tasked with tying wine themed ribbon on the neck of the bottle to give people the idea that wine makes a great gift. We chuckled at the idea that someone asks for a receipt for their wine and then takes it back if they didn't like drinking it. We laughed that that wouldn't ever happen, this wine was good. Write a "thank you" note after good. She even took her camera out of the tasting room one afternoon and got some lovely scenic shots of the building set in the vineyards.

While Josh and I got to know Riley, Betty came in one day

and said, "Hey friend! And they hugged. Henry, Ambrose, and Devin were all questioning, "You two know each other?" This is when we learned that Riley was hired based on Betty's recommendation. The two of them originally worked together at a trendy wine bar and restaurant on the main drag in Templeton. It was Betty's recommendation that got Riley the job. I was impressed to hear Betty had this type of pull already, and I wondered if I could get friends to work here too. Despite Riley being experienced in life, she was fresh-faced and more than once had a customer question, "Are you sure you're old enough to even work here?" She always replied with, "Yes, ma'am!"

It's no wonder her and Betty were work friends; they both knew the perfect way to put people who spoke before they thought, in their place. She was a nail biter yet always-always well-dressed. Once, the tasting room manager Tammy sent us on what she called "a work field trip" to learn about how other tasting rooms work. The winery she wanted us to see was couple miles away and we were told, like us, also focuses on Rhone blends. Well, that was the news to us as we didn't know we specialized in that, but I know I was happy to learn that. While at our field trip there, we were talking about getting lunch after. I enjoyed feeling like one of the girls and getting to know them. Riley mentioned she's gluten free, and thusly sensitive to the dietary needs of others. She asked the winemaker, "When I am talking to a customer, and they're vegan can I recommend these wines? Is wine vegan?" to which the man working there said "No."

This was a seemingly rhetorical question as we were there to wine taste and get the vibe of the place, but her question felt like she was trying to either challenge the wine educator, or make small talk, I couldn't exactly tell. He explained, that it's not and said, "Oh no, no, it's not vegan. They use animal products as part of the wine making process." I was shocked and wondered how on Earth that works because how can grape juice change, and ferment in a barrel and not be vegan. I felt united to the girls when we were all somehow all so surprised that we forgot to ask any follow up questions. We all vowed to never go vegan for the particular reason that we couldn't drink wine.

Back at Stonefruit Cellars, Riley loved to take customers on little walks in the backyard and into a few rows of vineyard to see the zinfandel and malbec's grape clusters forming. Henry knows this complex history of modern California zinfandel from Croatian plavac mali to Italian primitivo and taught us a few things when we overheard him with other customers. Out there in the vineyard, it was easy to gaze at the talkative and social magpies which seems to always be under the old oak trees. Customers loved her vineyard tours. They raved about seeing how grapes form from little green buds and then eventually flower ad get pollinated. After that, then these tiny flowers will become a grape. The vineyard was also intriguing when the grapes were full and ripe and juicy. Riley and I sometimes even let customers pull a few plump grapes off the vine so they could taste the juice for themselves. They often thought as though we gave them the greatest snack of all time. The acid and juicy combination was so different from the wine in their glass, everyone was fascinated by this little treat for the vineyard.

Seeing her success in wowing the customers, and getting tipped handsomely, a few others of us made vineyard tours part of our routine. It was a guaranteed way to educate customers who were smitten by our beautiful vineyard. On our lunch breaks, Riley always knew of the best hole-in-the-wall restaurants in Paso. She knew where to get pupusas delivered from, or that the bibimbap from Solo's way out on Creston Road served from the kindest of kind staff was worth the drive all the way from the tasting room.

SURPRISE ME

I was changing, adding a whole new world to my knowledge bank, and noticing how people are in a fun setting. I loved learning modern girlhood from Riley and Betty. I realized I was craving fun too. That was partially what drew me to this job. I was interested in the lively atmosphere of a busy bar. I also craved pushing my comfort zone, and being challenged. The customers often surprised me. The way one conversation between two would morph into a conversation across the bar to another and then another was a nice surprise. The vibe is definitely vibing when this happens. It's loud, but not in an annoying way, it's excitingly loud. We kept the music on a fairly low level, and did experiments as to what music is best received by customers. Feeling like we were in the live action version of the Three Little Bears. We had to find just the right music station. It couldn't be too hot, or to cool. It had to be just right.

We tried Apple Music, a commercial-free music service with different stations and playlists and played a station called Rock Hits, but it was too much base sometimes. We tried one called 90's Throwbacks, but it was too new and needed too much lyric editing in those hip hop and grunge songs. We tried a Jazz Melody station but it was too sleepy. The station that absolutely no one complained about was a Motown Station. It would either be tunes that snuck under the radar of people's conversations allowing them to talk and connect, or it was peppy and enjoyable enough that no one complained. Playing that station was always a dang good time. When the mood is high and happy in the tasting room, customers sometimes know to just make their requests fast so you can get them what they need quickly, and them move over to help others. They can do this by reminding me which taste on the menu they had last. I often ask, "How did you enjoy The Cab?" if I remembered what they just enjoyed, or could tell by the color in their glass, or they would tell me, "I'm ready for the Malbec, please." Both get the job done and keep them moving forward with the tasting menu.

It was pretty predictable that on any given weekend day in the summer that someone will say to me, "Surprise me!" when I ask them what I can get them from behind the bar. If this is accompanied with a smile, it's charming and welcomed. When it's said expectantly, I can tell that customer doesn't care what they're drinking, for this beverage's main purpose is simply to get them drunk. This is much less charming.

The camaraderie at the bar when it's busy and full of smiling patrons is so much fun. Time goes by faster when it's buzzing. Our feet are less sore from standing, as their smiles fulfill happiness deep within our souls. Even with the bustling atmosphere, we still notice things like smiles and tone in your voice, so be nice, and keep the good times coming.

Sometimes the fun extends from behind the bar. Servers and customers share a joke. The most popular joke is the one between server and customer about there being a whole in the bottom of the bottle, or plate where the drink or food has gone. It's cheesy but harmless. Just like Henry. He brings donuts into work to share with coworkers. What a gesture of cheesy admiration. Customers come, and stay, for Henry. He was a beloved part of Stonefruit Canyon, and his mildly raspy voice when he says, "Welcome to Stonefruit Canyon" shows his experience and years spent behind the bar. When guests are comfortable with their server, we would hear customers say "There must be a hole on the bottom of this glass somewhere, it's all gone," while lifting up the bottle and looking sad that they in fact had drunk the entire bottle themselves. We've heard so many of these industry jokes that a genuine laugh from a server is fairly hard to achieve. However, one afternoon, Josh smiles his crooked smile, pours a sip for a customer and says, "Here have a sip and tell me if it's good," while making eye contact with his customer. The customer sipped, and then said, "Just a sip from the top right? 'cuz we all know you put the poison on the bottom!" Josh laughed a cackle sort of laugh that makes his eyes crinkle in the corners. After his laugh he said, "Oh man that's a genuine laugh not just a 'server laugh' I haven't heard that joke before!" Thanks for coining the term, 'Server Laugh,' Josh. We needed a name for the fake laugh that gets us through many a long shift with copious, 'hole in the bottom of this glass' jokes.

RIDING THE HOG

From their sedan in the parking lot, we spy a heavyset man with a faded Harley Davidson shirt, and his wife with a sequined hobo bag and early 2000's capri pants make their way to the tasting room entrance. Just as they're about to reach out for the doorknob, Josh says, "These look like your people" and dips out, returning down the ramp to the back office to do paperwork. I greeted the couple, with a "Hello! Welcome to Stonefruit Canyon. I'm Jenn!" They walk up to the bar, and with a sigh of fatigue, plop their hands on the bar as if they are finally reaching their long-awaited destination.

I asked, "From where are you visiting us?" to initiate the conversation and the day is officially rolling. After exchanging pleasantries, the couple from Topeka is visiting their favorite city, Morro Bay, for the week. She says she's a fan of whites and rosé wine and he doesn't drink, citing new medications negatively interacting with all his new medication. They stand at the bar and look at the menu, a bit aware how early it feels at 10:30am and ask if they're the only ones there. I cheerfully tell them they in fact are and point out how this is a good thing as I can devote all my attention on them finding a wine they, well, the wife part of the duo loves. The husband strolls the tasting room and sees the small selection of coasters embedded with the winery's original logo, and a few logo button ups, and t-shirts faded from being in the window too long. I begin the flight of wines by pouring the Estate Chardonnay. Grown just miles from the tasting room, this wine is award winning and represents

Templeton Gap's effect on the grape. The woman smells it, and I begin my speech if you will, saying, "You may notice pale gold color and notes of citrus. It has a nose of honeysuckle and lemon and pairs well with fresh fruit, because of the new French oak it was casked in.

"It's subtle creaminess even allows it to be paired with popcorn, if that's the mood you're in,"

A moment later, the man plops on a bistro set's petite chair. The plop is loud enough to get my attention, and I notice he has a bag that's…moving. Now distracted from chardonnay education, I'm struck by seeing what initially I thought was a purse strap is actually a leash dangling from the purse. My eagle-eyes focus on the man, and his…living purse. The man looks down and his face tenders. And then, out of his bag pops the head of a little pig.

"Oops, wow! Who's that?" I said, and that's enough of an invitation in the man's eyes that he hoists the pig out of the bag and releases the it onto the floor. Its hooves are tiny, and I feel like too much of a city girl for this situation. There's a 'call for help from the backroom button' and I push it. When Josh emerges from the kitchen in a similar fashion as Kramer from Seinfeld, I say, "Friend, you've got to see this cutie and meet its people." Josh, being a country boy, is relieved it's not a *real* call for help, but more of a call to share, and says, "Cute, a Vietnamese pot-bellied pig!"

In shock now thinking, "There are types of pigs?" I try to return to normalcy and grabs the next selection from today's tasting flight and pour the next wine straight from the chilled fridge, for the woman wasn't as distracted as I was and gulped down her chardonnay sample quicker than I realized she was ready for the next taste.

As the woman, now under two sets of eyes, sipped her sample, I quietly asked Josh if pigs are actually allowed to be in the tasting room. He replies, "As long as Georgia the cat doesn't mind, neither do I." Georgia the winery cat was still on the tasting room's roof, so all was copasetic. Sensing that I could handle it from here, Josh returned to his desk in the backroom, and I wondered what kind of animal would be in here next time someone pushed the button to summon backup to the tasting room.

SPEAKING FROM EXPERIENCE

Tony was a tasting room customer who became a memorable regular. He stood on the left side of the bar every Saturday from about 11am to 3pm. He drove a different color and model Corvette each week. He wore broken in jeans and grey shirts whose material were so thin they were nearly see-through. This revealed he definitely worked out multiple times a week. He had tan skin that was closer to orange in the tasting room lighting. There were certain OCD-like behaviors during this visit that I noticed right away. For example, he would order one glass of cabernet sauvignon. No tasting flight as is customary with all patrons, just one glass of red wine, and it could only be cabernet sauvignon. Always, and only one glass of just that. He would sip it so very slowly to last the whole afternoon. He wouldn't leave the bar for much of anything, but when he did have to leave his post at the bar to talk to people about his car, he would happily oblige. Mostly because it would be a 20-something, looking for a hot post for their social media accounts. It was about half and half males and female who wanted a picture with his car. The car was beautiful being in the oh-so-Instagrammable bucolic background of the photo which featured rows and rows of grapevines and then Tony's classic, mint condition Corvette in the foreground. In this aesthetic-fueled environment, the shot must be as magnetic as imaginable. Plus, people were a bit braver to ask for a picture as they were drinking and often a tad less shy or embarrassed to be so focused on consumerism.

Although we did notice he was happier when it was a young female corvette fan, he would entertain anyone who talked to him. When leaving his wine to talk to a Corvette fan, he would place something as a coaster on top of his glass and wave that he'd be right back. We didn't have lightweight coasters so often he would use a Wine Club sign up booklet as a coaster. Always resourceful. What made Tony stand out even more was his age. Probably closer to 70, Tony's aptitude for cabernet and corvettes, and his tanned biceps didn't make him look a day over 50, in a way. In the 'if you're standing far away' way. The numbers game got more interesting as Tony always tipped a fresh $20 bill, over the cost of his glass of wine. You see, he was in our wine club, so his glass was comped on every visit, so it was just about the tip for this transaction. He entertained us workers with his stories over the four hours of nursing his wine, and these stories were other worldly. We learned that Tony used to be a bartender himself, and had theories about alcohol consumption. Namely, he believed in drinking only while standing. While Stonefruit Canyon offered plenty of comfortable seating options, Tony would only stand, citing his vertical behavior to the fact it helped him gauge his sobriety better. He had an enviable Corvette collection, and despite his routine behavior and charming idio-syncrasies, it's no wonder he was a Saturday favorite!

What wasn't predictable however was my coworker's reactions to his tips. Some would behave different and I felt myself behaving differently too. While his $20 tip was in line with his hourly time at the bar as it $5 per hour. Since he was taking up space there and no other tasters could be at that area, his $5 per hour tip balanced out the monopoly he had over that square-footage of the bar counter. However, with him not needing much attention from tasting room staff, it was easier to earn that $20 than tend to four different parties over those four hours. You see, he needed his wine poured and coaster set out for him, and he needed a little 'hello' and commentary about his car choice of the day or the weather, but Tony didn't require explanation of the wines or regional terroir (the characteristics of soil which effect the grapevine). So, this fairly easy to earn tip sent tasting room staff into strategic modes. We would behave differently, like savages for money. Some would take their lunch break before 11am, insuring they could be the one to welcome Tony and pour wine for him. Others, who missed their chance at the beginning of his stay, would chat throughout the time there and linger at the end, hoping to be the one to ring him up- insuring a place for themselves as the tip keeper. We looked out for each other, but at times we competed with each other. Money had that kind of influence on us.

SLOW SEASON

O ur tasting room manager was all about collaborating with other businesses. He had organized a female-owned coffee truck that would park in our parking lot in the early morning. The truck would capitalize on our location that many drove past on their way to work. Catering to the early morning commuters taking the highway 46W Eastbound and Westbound that connected Paso to Cambria. The Coffee Truck was basically like a food truck, but they only specialized in coffee beverages. The owners hoped the same customers would stop by for wine on their way home from work. I didn't really realize how many people make that commute uncaffeinated before the truck set up shop. As someone who enjoys coffee, I was glad to hear of this new partnership as I could get a second coffee in the mornings after arriving to work.

This was nice for a few weeks, but us morning shift workers noticed a pattern. When the truck closed for the day, usually around 10:30AM, as most commuters were gone and the tasting room was about to open, a certain aroma would be left behind. You see, the entrepreneur running the truck also negotiated that she could use our bathroom in the tasting room as her truck wasn't equipped with one. She was so busy her only bathroom break came after working. So when the truck closed and after drinking coffee for hours, a very natural thing occurred. Well, as any avid coffee drinker knows what coffee does to our bowels in the morning, you can assume you understand correctly. The aroma of evidence was left behind and in the relatively small area of the tasting room, there was no mystery as to what happened in the bathroom moments ago. This is distasteful under normal circumstances, but in a tasting room where we rely on our sense of smell to enjoy the wine for all that it is, the partnership with the poop truck, I mean coffee truck, needed to end. Thankfully, customers came a bit after our 11 AM opening time which gave us workers just enough time to open all the windows, and laugh our asses off, before the first customers came in to our newly fresh-as-a-daisy tasting room.

RED OR WHITE

J osh was an interesting kind of guy who would get to work early to make sure everything was ready for guests. At times, this was unexpected as he also gave off the party-boy vibe. Josh is paradoxical and intoxicating. He was something to sober up from. I am sure many women did. He'd been given special tours around many an AirBnBs, usually by pretty women who visited the tasting room during the day. Being a sleepy town, visitors may need something to entertain themselves as tasting rooms close at 5PM. Anyone coming to Paso on a quest to use all five senses in Paso would be intrigued by Josh. Coming in to work early showed he understood that putting in the time early made everything run smother during the day. He preferred early preparation over staying late the night before which makes sense as he has places to be and things to do. I find it's much easier to work ahead and prepare for the next day than have to come in in the early morning and have do the work hungover, but to each his own.

He never said it aloud, but he was a planner. He'd have the glasses polished and the syrah stocked. Then, he'd go a step beyond. He would prepare for the day by looking up events in the area to find out if there was a charity bike ride or antique fair happening, as the tourists often spill into the tasting rooms after those kinds of events. Preparation and research served to make him undistracted by tasks and good at connecting with people. In the tasting room you never know who is going to walk through the doors and all sorts of people over 21 years of age find themselves at places like Stonefruit Canyon. Despite his young age, Josh could handle all kinds of different types of people with ease. He could talk to anyone. The time talking at the bar in between sips of wine, of course, is what solidifies the tasting room experience. Simply put, he was charming, and charismatic and despite the fact he retold jokes, his punchlines still haven't gotten old to me. I wonder if my attraction to him was becoming obvious to others, or to him. I sure hope not.

He was the son of a restaurant owner in town, and like most coastal country boys, he loves trucks. His big truck, which he expectedly named, "Big Red," is one of the things that he smiles his big full smile for. His face stands out at the top of his lanky, yet strong lean physique. His crooner voice is exaggerated by his habit of talking low and close to your ears. This habit of being a close talker has the tendency to establish a quick intimacy as it feels he's talking just to you. I loved listening to him explain wine terms to me. He taught me about, "bottle shock" which is a wine term of something that can happen right when the wine leaves the barrel and goes into the bottle. He explained to me, "This transfer includes the process of filtration, and the wine may touch the air causing a tad bit of oxidation to occur. Although, thankfully this is a temporary condition, and the wine will settle down and be its tasty self again." Josh adds that "Winemakers shouldn't be scared of switching things up because the wine was ready for the bottle but may just not know it yet." He's insightful, and metaphorical at times.

Like a golden retriever with a ball, he went and went and went. Like all creatures, he eventually lands and has, on occasion, fallen asleep at his desk after late nights out. He didn't struggle to find a date. There's plenty of those as his boyish charm and party persona mixed with his slow country mannerisms made him come across as harmless. At home, he cared for livestock, mainly cows and goats, on his family's property. He does excellent Russian accents, and is full of surprises. Always a clever guy, he worked around some county rules and instead of mowing back the grass that grows on the land, he found a loophole in the rules that make him not have to mow the grass as what's growing is considered animal feed rather than weeds. This means he's growing food for his animals and not just letting his land get taken over by weeds. This clever practice bypasses the city's rule of cutting back growth every spring, which is a rule to limit dry brush in this warm summer climate. He was close to the tasting room manager, Tom. Tom is very much unlike Josh. He had severe social anxiety and mostly stays in the tasting room's backroom office space. Tom does leave his mousehole to go bicycling locally. When Tom travels, Josh housesits for him. I figured out that Josh is like a son to Tom. Housesitting is such a college student gig, but he fits the look. Josh is a young, single, heart-breaker. He would probably survive a Zombie apocalypse with his nimble nature and tenacity. He didn't large gauge piercings in his ears, but if he did, he'd definitely have wine corks in the holes. He lived and breathed Paso wine.

RAPPORT AND REPOUR

I n the tasting room as we got to talking between sips, we wine educators will talk about the wine some, and then about your travel there, your visit, and the conversation can go anywhere from there. The goal is personal connection, as that's where the magic happens. The magic feels like being with someone who instantly likes you. It's like being a dog in human form who thinks everyone is their new best friend. To be liked by someone who doesn't know you, sure feels different than being known and unliked. This was one of the lessons I was learning in this second coming of age I was going through. I loved the chats with customers, but being accepted as one of the team brought more meaning into every conversation and I realized it was something I didn't know I'd been craving. Tapping into this kind of instant friendship magic erases all discomfort with small talk. Yeah, we talked about the weather but we also talked about our relationships, and money worries. We joked about there being too much month at the end of money. We shared which urgent care facility best helped our kids when they got sick. Maybe my soul had met these people already, or needed to meet these people in this space.

We were all unofficially trained on the job. Our "grandpa" Henry did a lot of this for us, as he'd been working there the longest. He has been there when all of us experienced our first day. He modeled that we should encourage customers to "savor their sips." I wanted to savor each sip. I wanted to savor life, so I listened to him as if his words were gospel. He used this time to do what Henry does best — tell a story. He's a patient storyteller, meaning he's slow and lets his talking take up the space so the person at the bar has time to sip on their wine sample for a few good minutes. I notice this also gives customers time to come up with a question, or comment back to Henry. Henry already understands that the majority of even the most seasoned wine drinkers don't go wine tasting every day, so he knows to give them time to help it be a special experience for them. Henry would woo his customers into his aura by saying things like, "Wine is spiritual, or perhaps just a qusai-spiritual experience" and while we'll never quite know if Henry is quoting a Wine Enthusiast magazine article, or a wee bit tipsy himself, it's true. Wine can be spiritual. Heck, it's mentioned in the bible by name 190 times. It's used in many religious rights of passages and drank on communion as some believe it represents the blood of Christ. The way customers would connect with Henry and nod in agreement is similar to parishioners in the pews at church. He was good with people, well-spoken, and told customers something in a way that makes them believe it. He was the prophet helping earn the winery a profit.

I wanted to be able to do this too. I noticed it's also what Pablo said in the Forbes training. It's all about making a connection. Both hail from Vermont? Connection. Both Green Bay Packers fans? Connection. Both left-handed. Connection. The wine educator is having this connection with you on one end of the bar, and a connection with someone else at the other end of the bar. Sometimes the stories combine, and a momentary scene from the old school television show Cheers takes place. To get the whole bar full of patrons talking is a moment of magic. When this happens, it is great for guests as they make friends and chat together, and this chatting gives a moment of reprieve for the wine educator as well. This reprieve from entertaining gives them a chance to maintain their bar's tidiness. They can fill this space with polishing wine glasses, restocking bottles that have sold, and wiping down the area from previous guests. This unique connection made due to happenstance can make people fall in love, so to speak, with the pourer and the winery as a whole. When this happens, many people show appreciation with their gratuity, or, tip, but sometimes they love it so much they want to be a part of the winery. This is when people decide to join a winery's wine club. This is a contract commitment to buying wine a few times a year and it's in the winery's interests because it guarantees them repeat customers and in the wine drinker's interests because it ensures that they get the wine they like before it sells out. Plus, there are often pickup parties where the club members attend an exclusive party at the winery. The winery often closes early to host these pickup parties and it allows the member to feel valued. They get to mingle with like-minded wine lovers and bring home their allotment of wine that they pre-purchased. If they can't attend the party, their wine is shipped to them, bringing their connection to the winery to their doorstep. This keeps the rapport going as wine drinkers get to pour and repour their favorite wine at home; the connection sustains.

DEAD HEAD

My coworker Ambrose is a music lover and UCLA graduate, giving prep school vibes. With prior jobs such as former speech writer in Washington and old book reseller, he most definitely listens to NPR. He's currently in relationship with a woman who looks like she's out of a 90's United Colors of Benetton advertisement. As her baby daddy, he walks the part of East Coast prep with a quiet air of luxury about him. He wore vintage Ralph Lauren and J. Crew, nearly exclusively. I say nearly, as he did wear a dancing bear hat sometimes, as he loves the Grateful Dead. Despite the 45-minute commute from home, he wanted this particular job so he doesn't have to take his work home with him. He gets fired up from the day's happenings enough as is and feels having a long commute in which he smokes weed provides the balance he needed. His "Welcome to Stonefruit Canyon, I'm Ambrose!" was lilting, inviting people in with his upbeat confidence.

Him and Josh make a great pair, despite their differences in being raised by the city or the country. They both are nice to me, and I imagine Ambrose would be great to go vintage shopping with. He certainly has an eye for style. His accessory choices were stellar. Loafers, cuffed chinos, and a dad hat all together in a very cool manner. It was interesting how he wore preppy clothes and looked effortlessly cool, whereas our manager Tammy wore preppy clothes too and looked uncomfortable. I thought about how much an extra done up button really did that to someone's look. It was such a small button, but I noticed that's what changed their looks. Riley wore similar slacks, but the fabric was more something that came from Express than Ralph Lauren. That's what made her style different. It was something small that changed the vibe. Fabric is magic in that it conveys such different vibes. I was feeling very observant about my own body and clothes. I wondered if there was a difference between wearing and styling, my clothes, and if I was doing it right. What even is "right" anyway, I wondered. These people made me so curious about them, and myself. One day, when we're all working together and Josh is behind the bar, he was frantically looking around the notepads and cards and looks up and asked, "Where's my favorite pen?" I reply with a little giggle and smile, "Josh, you're too young to have a favorite pen." He really was such an old soul in how he behaved, having claimed a pen at work as his favorite, and all. It was cute to me how he thought those sorts of things were important. It was the first time seeing how valuable pens are when working in customer service. I took note of this, and always had a pen in my left back pocket so I could make friends by lending them something they needed. I thought to myself that Ambrose probably ran a pen factory in college, or smuggled cocaine onto a plane in a pen's center cavity. He always had an outlandish story to tell, and we all liked that about him as he could entertain us while we polished wine glasses.

ADRIAN

One Saturday I was working with Josh, and at around noontime we saw Adrian's dark blue BMW bring up a cloud of sand in the parking lot. Josh goes, "Oh there's my friend! Haha." I wondered what he meant, specifically, I wonder what his friends are like and who he's talking about as a glimpse into Josh's world so to speak. It's only my first few weeks at Stonefruit Canyon, so I am getting comfortable in always expecting something interesting to happen. No two days were the same around here.

It was a busy Saturday and I was used to hearing that even on busy days, we'd have a few regular customers. I already knew that we'd be likely to have Tony on our left of the bar and now I was meeting Adrian, who would apparently take up regular residence to the right of the bar. Adrian originally started off as Josh's customer, and during their first interaction, Josh signed Adrian up for the wine club after getting him to fall in love with the wine. Josh pitched it based on the allure of the location and hope to make new local friends. Adrian was new in town and originally went to Stonefruit Cellars as a third wheel to his friend's Ugly Sweater Party that was held at the winery. Wanting to put down roots in the Paso area, Adrian started coming to the winery sporadically on Saturdays. He drove a shiny blue BMW M4 two-door coupe and it kicked up a lot of dust in the parking lot. Josh quickly debriefed me about Adrian as he walked in from his car, "His presence was big since the first time he came in. After tasting, he would likely buy a couple bottles to gift to his best friends who lived nearby. He had just returned from a trip with them to Ireland when I met him. He loves whiskey, having toured the factory and made his own blend of Irish Whiskey. Having done the whiskey circuit, he came here wanting to learn about wine."

Adrian parked and walked into the tasting room. Josh walked out from behind the bar, and approached Adrian, giving him one of those man hugs combined with a fist bump. I was tending to my other customers and about to wrap it up with them. Needing a new customer, and going with the unspoken rule that men pour wine for women customers, and women pour for men customers, Josh leans to me and says, "Jenn, I want you to pour for my friend Adrian here. He's a good guy. He's in our wine club. Treat him well."

I smiled and placed a menu in front of him. I say that I would love to pour wine for him, and I thank Josh for the new customer as I had just settled up with my other group. I got Adrian a glass, and placed it in front of him. I walked to the refrigerator, grabbed the white wine that's first on the tasting menu and said, "Here's his first taste of the day — our viognier." Thankful for that high school French class again, I say those words confidently and smile. I mention the smell of apricot and peach on the nose, then pause to add in, "Oh maybe you already had this one when you were in last...When was that? I ask because we change the menu often."

He says it's been a few weeks as he got busy with work stuff. I continued on saying the wine has a beautiful minerality note to it as it's casked in concrete instead of oak barrels. He asks if they make concrete barrels, and I do my best to explain it how it was briefly told to me, that the winemaker used a concrete lined barrel that's in the shape of an egg. The concrete doesn't add an oaky flavor as a wooden barrel would and sometimes people enjoy this 'clean' basic flavor more.

He sips and I notice he savors his sips. He smells the wine in the glass before sipping it. He's not in a rush to get to his next winery. It feels as if this is his destination for the day. He doesn't gulp. He doesn't do that annoying thing when people try to help the server pour the wine into the glass where they hold the glass and move it to meet the bottle. He watches me pour the wine, and lets me do my thing. As a newly professional liquid pourer, I am still not a mind-reader predicting where someone will move that glass to. It's so awkward when I have to move the bottle around as a customer is moving their glass. I am thankful he's making this tasting easy on me. One point for Adrian!

With our bar generally being very busy from the opening hour to closing hour, having a friendly-faced man at the end of the bar really helps. He really can talk to anyone by the fact he's already got himself into a deep conversation about Marvel with the couple next to him. When I return from lunch, the three of them are still taking. I love being the silent listener instead of facilitating the conversation with my part of the bar. He is the type of guy who believes in making eye contact when you say "Cheers!" Adrian is friendly and quite a storyteller but he's never loud with his giggling and never hoots and hollers. He never pulls a Miles from Sideways and makes a scene. The way he can communicate with others about anything from travel airline points, to Star Wars makes him welcome to stay for hours. This lessens our load having to hold a conversation with the customer for the entire time it takes for them to enjoy their tasting, which often is about an hour. The most excited he was the first time I poured him a sip of the cabernet sauvignon. The play on words with the word divine is cutesy as it's wine from the vine, de vine. At this point in time, I am pouring the 2015 vintage and I've learned this is when the grapes were picked — autumn harvest of 2015. The tasting menu describes the wine as opening "with playful aromas of eucalyptus, mint, cassis, and cheery, with just a hint of warm cedar. Well-integrated tannins and balanced acid on the palate come together with touches of mocha, followed by a smooth, fresh finish." He liked it. The wine must have made quite an impression too, as after he swallowed the sip, he looked me direct in my eyes and asked, "Wow that is SO good, will you marry me? Wow!" and we chuckled together. I said, "It's a cabernet sauvignon, it's not a Love Potion."

I reached for the next bottle to pour from — the 2015 cabernet syrah. It's a unique blend as it's partially a Bordeaux style red mixed with a Rhone style red. It's something only the renegades of Paso could get away with. The tasting notes call it "a careful combination which creates a bouquet of flowers and clove on the nose. Then rich tannins spring forth on the palate with notes of strawberry and baking spices." I had just learned from Henry that we share a similar climate as France, and thus can grow the same varietals, or types of grapes. So, I explained that information to Adrian when I poured the wine for him. I was so proud that I had handled this tasting flight in a way that made myself feel proud. What a unique feeling. A magical feeling. All my curiosity made me learn about the winery, and I was able to teach it back to good customers. My curiosity sparked their curiosity. Wonder was contagious. I felt I deserved a "make shit happen" trophy, as this was something all my hard work was finally giving me.

DO GOOD

There's something about working a job where you don't know what the day will bring. There's no such thing as routine in a tasting room. Every day was different. But there is cyclical routine in the city with all the events held annually. In Paso, there's an annual fundraising tradition of having animals from Zoo to You, a local wild animal rescue, visit different wineries in the area. This is a spring tradition that coincides with the beginning of the busy season. It's a fundraiser for the animals who live at the nonprofit just outside of city limits. To participate, customers buy a Wine Safari Passport and then they use the passport as a pre-paid way to taste wine from different places. Then those participating travel from winery to winery sipping wine and meeting various rescued animals and hearing their backstory. This industry of wine and fundraising have something in common, I noticed. We're both in the businesses of crafting experiences. This year, at Stonefruit Canyon, a unique experience was crafted when a camel named Bugaboo visited. Riley asked, "If they have a lot of animals they care for, why did we get a camel?" We were told that the tasting room was assigned this camel as our parking lot was right next to the grassy area a large animal, like the camel Bugaboo, could easily be unloaded onto and they would be comfortable for hours. Not only was I working with a bunch of wild humans and two adorable cats, a literal animal was at the winery today too. I wanted my son to come see the camel at mommy's work, but my son and his dad were kayaking on a lake nearby. My son's dad had purchased a kayak on my first weekend at this job, about 12 weeks prior, and they finally were taking it out. I was worried that because my son wasn't a strong swimmer, this was a risky move. However, my son's dad said that I should get over my worry and that they would be fine without me. I poured myself into my work to distract me from my life at home. I was a bit skeptical how this camel day would be fun enough to distract me, but I quickly learned that there are many reasons to love a camel. One of Bugaboo's caregivers explained it this way, "Dromedary camels were the first domesticated animal nine thousand years ago. They were used for transportation, their wool, and lactose-free milk. They self-shed wool that's easily combed, and conveniently, their poop works as fire-starters. They can transport 3 people at a time, go a week without eating, and days without drinking. They can carry five times as much as a horse can their delivery service is better than a horse because they can sit on the ground and it's lower than a horse, so it's easier to load and unload. You can ride them by putting saddles on them, or you can simply bareback behind the hump. They are faster than a horse, you see this in the camel racing. They are built for their environment as they can close their nose to keep sand out. When sitting, they are essentially a wall that their riders can hide behind during a sandstorm."

My coworker and wine educator Ambrose added something even more surprising to the conversation when he said, "Oh I love camels, I would ride them when I worked in Egypt!" as he petted Bugaboo's long curved furry neck. I wondered, how does one go from working in Egypt to working in sleepy Paso Robles. I asked, and learned that Ambrose's talent with the written word got him working as a professional speech writer in Washington D.C. This kind of work took him on missions all over other parts of Africa as well. He still uses those skills when he speaks with customers. Normally he doesn't get to pet their necks though.

NINA

If you're familiar with the term Sugar Mama or Sugar Daddy, then you'll understand the friend version of the term, 'Sugar Bestie.' Nina is Betty's Sugar Bestie. Nina would financially care for Betty by footing the bill when they went out to dinner and stuff like that. They both were single mamas who had each other's back. They were each other's village. She was also what some would call a "bringer" meaning she's a social gal who is always bringing her friends wherever she goes. This is great for the bar scene that Stonefruit Canyon often was. Nina and her friends insured the vibe of the room was fun, flirty, and very social. I met so many of her friends who had time to come to the tasting room mid-day for a free glass of wine and chat, while talking to one of their besties, Betty. Nina is a daily patron at the tasting room, and shared that she is an Army Veteran. By the way she speaks, I imagine she has definitely seen some shit. I don't know much about the military except from watching GI Jane and Forrest Gump, so I am fascinated by her. She doesn't wear the PTSD I imagine she undoubtedly has on her face, as it hasn't hardened her in that way. Instead, she carried what she's gone through as sage wisdom. She as beautiful as she is resilient. I learned that she's been through a lot, since, well, forever. Since being adopted five times as a young child, to joining the military at a young age, she now is a no-holds-bar type of woman who has her hands full raising a young daughter. When she visits, she either drives a Range Rover or a GMC truck, depending on the day. Once, I asked her why she needs a big truck like that, and she told me, "Look, Jenn, I don't want to have to rely on anybody. I got the truck for autonomy." Damn, with an answer like that I think she's a queen too, and I really admire her.

I was learning the whole dance behind the bar. I knew where the whites and rosé wine was stored in the fridge in the mid-bar area, and I knew where the glasses were and how to bend discreetly when wearing a low cut top. I learned how to do the arm raises, just right, when pouring wine so I wouldn't pour too much. It was becoming a muscle memory now. This felt so great, but I still walked through life yearning and striving, and so curious. To hear Nina talk about wanting autonomy, and buying a truck for that purpose, I heard a woman with a plan make something for herself, just the way she wanted it. I hoped the dance of life, going from here to there, and handing it all with grace would be second nature to me soon too. I wanted my movements to be as memorized and taken in as who I am, as much as my behind-the-bar muscle memory was formed day-by-day, too. I promised myself one day my badassery would be second nature like Nina's.

REGULARS

B etty's personality had gained her some regulars to the
tasting room. Regulars meant they are customers who
come to the tasting room very often. These regulars though,
came to see her, primarily, and enjoy the wine as an added
bonus. Betty seemed to know when they're coming as they call
ahead and ask for her to pour wine for them. The word "they" is
a bit generous as the male of the duo is more hands off in the
tasting room, almost a token presence to his wife who always
takes the lead. With her in charge, they regularly buy at least
eight cases of wine each visit. Now remember that a case has 12
bottles of wine, so this was 96, nearly 100 bottles of wine a few
times a year! I was fascinated by their relationship in which the
woman appeared to be making all of the decisions. She never
consulted her husband about his preferences on anything. This
was so different from how boyfriends and I interacted. I was
raised by a 1950's style housewife whose opinion came second
to her husband's highly regarded opinions.

One time Betty asked the couple of regulars what their vacation was like, and found out that Stonefruit Canyon wasn't the
only winery they shopped at when coming on vacations to Paso
Robles. Betty gushed this to us in the break room with all of us
working, and it really boggled our minds! We had a lot of questions for them, well for Betty as we wanted her to ask certain
things for us. We learned that because of the fact they can't ship
the wine home to themselves as they're from Utah, and their

state government limits alcohol being sent to their state, the couple did road trips here to bring the contrabanded goods back home over the border. During one of their afternoon visits in late summer we got to thinking about how much wine they were buying and how they can't be drinking that much per day and it dawned on us. Adding up their behaviors, it was clear enough to Betty that they are Polygamists. Everything added up and made sense now! They had travelled from Utah, and while here, they were stocking up on copious amount of wine to bring back to their home. Given this hunch, and her natural ability to be upfront, Betty got nosy one time, and started acting as if she knew, and understood their lifestyle. She point blankly asked the woman of the duo how their relationship works. Betty's rapport with them must have been strong enough that the woman didn't deny the polygamy and instead added that each of the sister wives have different interests and their husband takes them each on a trip that's of interest to them. To her it was California wine that sparked her interest, and made great souvenirs for the ladies back home. Betty told me they're excellent tippers on top of being excellently interesting, and because they have established such a rapport by coming in to the tasting room when Betty was there, they have shared further. Betty learned that they own a successful body care company based in the outskirts of Salt Lake City which made lavish trips like this all possible. When work gets tough on some days, Betty teased that she considered joining their multi-relationship to escape it all. But we all know she is too loyal to the cities of Templeton and Paso to really make that much of a life leap.

I took stories of this couple in and was jealous, admittedly. I wanted a husband to take me on trips. I wanted a large souvenir budget. The idea of sharing my husband was less than desirable, but I figured one fifth of a husband was better than nothing. I also wondered what my sister wives would bring home for me from their trip with our husband. Would having a sister wife be like having a roommate, or, best friend? How do they make peace with all the versions of their husbands lives? I was left with so much curiosity and noticed that more I knew about people, the more I wanted to learn about them. But first, I had to learn about myself, and make peace with all the versions of me.

49%

One day when the sons of the winery owners Liam and Sean stopped by the tasting room, they were talking about now that they were nearly in charge, they could begin decorating and redoing parts of the tasting room and production facility. Their word "nearly" made me incredibly curious. I saw Georgia peeking in at the door, wanting to be let in, and I went over to open the door for her. When I did that, I overheard the brothers who were saying they're only 49% owners and the parents owned the other 51%. This explained their "nearly" comment, as well as how their partners were now getting to be involved with the aesthetics of the place. Both of their better halves were very talented with interior design and with floral design, and this was a blank slate for that particular kind of artistry. From what I could tell their entire family was so artistically talented. The boys made wine, and the women made the environment. What a perfect power couple pairing. Earlier that year, they had revamped one of the two rental units, called cottages, on Stonefruit Canyon's properties. While they were all chatting on the far side of the bar area, I overheard that our tasting room manager, Tammy, had moved into one of the cottages closest in the largest vineyard. I could see how this was convenient for her, and she was very involved in the winery. However, I felt this would instantly reduce the revenue the winery could make, as it had rented for hundreds of dollars a night, AirBnB style. Plus, with her occupying the property, it was one less perk us wine educators could offer special guests.

There wasn't another cottage I could offer guests. Us wine educators were using the place as a perk when signing up people for our wine club. With one less perk to offer, I would potentially be losing out on money. I received a commission for signing people up for the club his worried me a little as I'd have to rework my wine club pitch to not include the cottage property. Knowing the owners were hands on and loved meeting fans of their wine, I could be particularly convincing when I promised that as a wine club member, they would likely be able to receive a hands-on vineyard tour and even eat some eggs from the owner's own chickens. My tasting room guests who wanted to rub shoulders with the winery owners always became wine club members when I told them this perk's detail. I still worried my sales pitch would need revamping after overhearing this update though.

The Stonefruit Canyon proprietor, Mr. Heck, liked socializing and talking with guests. For a moment, it seemed on the surface that he may have had a favorite guest in allowing Tammy to live there, but in reality, his workload was lightened when they didn't have to hire a cleaning crew to clean up between the guests staying overnight in the cottage. Plus, her living there, I assume, provided a very consistent income as her rent would be year-round and would definitely be there during the winter months, when tourism to Paso slowed a little bit. I see how this was a win-win situation for everyone involved, but personally, I was very curious about renting the other cottage on the property. I desperately wanted to take the big leap and leave the complicated relationship I had with my son's dad. I was desperate for the change in my home life. So much so that I would have asked about it then and there, but I was privy to overhearing their conversation, and didn't feel like outing myself that I overhead these kinds of details. The timing unfortunately wasn't right to ask for such a job perk. It's not like the place was listed on Craigslist or something. I had overheard the conversation how the exception was made for the tasting room manager. I was only part time, but four days a week was the most I could work as I was piecing together childcare from my parents and my son's dad who offered to babysit on Saturday and Sunday. Despite not being able to work full time, I really wanted to be like Tammy and have an exception made for me too. I had been saving all my cash tips and had quite a stockpile to pay first and last months' rent on my own place. I just had to seek and find the exact right opportunity for myself, my son, and our dog Luna. I would have to come up with another way to launch the new life. In the meantime, I would be like the Heck girls and dreamed of how I could decorate my own place until I had a place 100% to myself. One thing I knew for certain: there would be flowers everywhere.

"You people. You think you can just buy your way into this. Take a few lessons. Grow some grapes. Make some good wine. You cannot do it that way. ... You have to have it in your blood. You have to grow up with the soil underneath your nails, and the smell of the grape in the air that you breathe. The cultivation of the vine is an art form. The refinement of its juice is a religion that requires pain and desire and sacrifice." - Gustavo, *Bottle Shock* (2008 Film)

GRAPE TALKING TO YOU

The world of wine was such a big thing here in Paso there were even radio shows about it. Alex Hill had a podcast and radio show on The Harvest. The show is called Grape Talk. Alex gets himself in the coolest wine situations and gets to interview who's who in Paso. I thought of myself as a student in this area. I choose to read books and watch movies about wine, so it was natural to listen to the radio show too. I was particularly interested in tuning in when they were interviewing the owners of Stonefruit Canyon, some of the OGs in the area: the Heck family. They discussed how their winery was a family business, and how the proverbial torch passing would be happening soon. They were not for sale, but would work to keep all the wine success in the family. Even though the winery was started over 40 years ago, it was still relevant as a top producer in the area today. I was so relieved that what I overheard last week was public knowledge. I hated keeping secrets.

Later during the show, my ears perked up like a dog when when it hears the word "treat" when Alex mentioned 420 Cellars' labeling. Alex called the winery owners, "geniuses of their innuendo." He was referring to their labels that were pushing the envelope of what's allowed on store shelves, which is highly regulated. Alex referenced the exact same Ask Me Nicely wine bottle that got me interested in the wine industry in the first place. I felt so connected and part of something big. It was on the radio after all, it was big. Alex also credited the Heck family for, "staking their claim to zinfandel grapes in the early

1980's" and how their success was a "right time, right place, kinda thing." I was inspired by the notion of this. That the winery owners were opportunists too. I felt a kindred spirit connection to them even further when they talked about being school teachers in their past. I had that in common with them to, and felt I was in the right place at the right time.

Alex loved talking about wine, and pointed out how zinfandel is a grape with juice that is high alcohol but not a lot of structure. It's a wine that's fun and affordable. Now, from having experience pouring their wine for months, I knew that Stonefruit Canyon currently produced 9 different zinfandel wines; two for distribution, meaning they were shipped all over the world, and the other 7 which were exclusively sold in the tasting room.

Also introduced was the Heck's business partner Tyler. He said that marketing the wine has been incredibly easy, "Getting Stonefruit Canyon in to different wineries and restaurants just works. People are friendly and the dynamic is special and precious." I thought, *God being likable is paying off for them.* Tyler, added that since Stonefruit Canyon is known as an 'old vine zin house' they focus on a lot of estate growing, and vines that are old, which in the industry means over 100-years old, and direct to consumer sales, which are hands-on experience driven. The hands-on experience he was referencing was all of us in the tasting room. The one's pouring the wines. The ones educating the customers. I felt slated that the team's effort was reduced to the phrase, "hands-on experience driven" and the human side was taken out if it. We mattered. Our work mattered, but to Tyler we were an aspect in a PowerPoint, or worse, an Excel spread-sheet. This was the first time I felt less than, while at work here. The owners, all 100% of them, were always so lovely to me. They made me feel like a whole person, not just a glorified dish-washer, which I felt like I was from closing time on when we cleaned all the wine glasses we served our customers throughout the day. I calmed myself by doing some yoga inspired ujjayi breathing and reminded myself the smart Heck family hired this guy to sell the wine. He was probably so good at his job that Stonefruit Canyon would earn a positive world class reputation, and line iteming my experience there on my resume would eventually help my life for the better.

Mr. Heck closed the interview with something that really was food for thought. He added that, "After being in the industry so long, it's been a challenge to get small, just as it was a challenge to get big." I certainly felt big and small at the same time. I felt small as I was just learning about this larger winery production scene, I really hasn't seen a glimpse of as I worked in the tasting room. But I also felt big, as I was becoming a big part in the world of Paso wine.

WORK HARD PLAY HARD

As a reward to the team for high sales and high accolades in customer service, the tasting room closed on a traditionally slow day in February to do a bit of team building and to thank us for all our work in the past year. The tasting room staff was told we would be paid for this day as usual, and we would be with the production team and office staff as well, hence the team building intent. When the long-awaited day came, I got to the tasting room and saw many people standing in the parking lot by the famously big chair at the entrance, a black luxury van parked nearby. I didn't recognize many others aside from the owners of the winery. Soon after I arrived, more familiar coworkers arrived. I was always chronically early places. Our tasting room manager, Tammy, was pacing in the parking lot. She had a soft-sided cooler bag with her and said this had our lunch in it. My Spidey-sense went into full gear as there was already 15 or so people gathered to board the bus, and I wondered how that many lunches were in that bag. I reminded myself that we were getting paid for this day no matter what, and it was supposed to be fun, so I talked myself out of worrying. We loaded up on the bus and I purposefully sat towards the front of the bus so I wouldn't get carsick, as I'm apt to do. Our day began with a tour of a winery also on the west side of Paso. They welcomed us in their production facility and it was nice. I mean niiiice and nicer than Stonefruit Canyon. They offered us a glass and sip of their cabernet as we began to tour and walk around the facility. They showed us their barrel room, which was giant. We

TASTING ROOM CONFIDENTIAL

went to their tasting room and tried a second wine and sat down on a big wooden table they use for hosting tastings for big parties. I sat next to Betty. Josh and Henry sat behind us, and Devin sat alone in the row behind them.

Our next to-do was to load back up in the bus and Tammy handed out water bottles for each of us. She also handed out a package of salami, and told us to take one and pass it around. Take a salami, like a piece. I thought to myself, this would be a long day of tummy rumbles, if this was the lunch they planned. Luckily, our next stop came soon. It was to another winery and we went straight to their tasting room after all unloading from the bus. Walking into this tasting room was an experience like no other. It was panning out to be more formal and contrived. Things were new and shiny. I felt like an actor in the commercial for the winery. I got suspicious of this when the owner and wine-maker taught us about how they turned grapes into wine. This was not supposed to be training. It wasn't supposed to make us see the other greener grass at other wineries. We were told this was an award for a job well done, but the vibe was so off.

The winery owner continued to pitch themselves to us in an effort to have us recommend our customers check out their place next in their day of wine tasting. While this sounds like a good business idea, it backfired as they were elitist feeling and too far removed from our humble former one room schoolhouse tasting room at Stonefruit Canyon. If our Stonefruit Canyon tasters complained about the $10-15 tasting flight fees, then recommending a place that's $45+ per tasting flight and only available with advanced reservations, isn't going to work for our typical customers and we all seemed to feel the same awkwardness.

By the looks of her expressions, Betty was obviously also perturbed by the lack of food on this trip so far. She reached into her black faux-leather crossbody purse and grabbed a snack. While munching on the sandwich, I put my attention on her. "Betty, where did you get that sandwich?" I asked. She looked me in the eyes, smiled a small smile, and said, "Jenn, it's my purse sandwich." A purse sandwich. A freakin' purse sandwich! I had never even considered the idea of that before and was intrigued and wondered why on Earth I hadn't thought of it before now. I also wondered why I had trusted a very petite skinny woman to pack enough snacks for all of us in the first place. I wished I thought of making myself a purse sandwich like Betty did. I admire her so much and was always humbled by her ideas to care for herself. I knew I still had a lot to learn from her.

Our next stop was down a long windy dirt road on the West Side of Paso. Have you ever noticed how "windy" like the weather and "windy" like a curvy road are the same? It's kind of cute when you think about it being pronounced "wine-dy" as there was so many grapevines growing on this road and tasting rooms scattered throughout. We stopped in the middle of an elevated field and got out in the soil that had mushy puddle spots. It looked rough and had tiny sprigs growing in rows. The partial owner of Stonefruit Canyon, Liam, explained that this was his new land, for his new winery and these sprigs are what new grapevines look like. He mentioned how there were a few challenges with this land, namely rodents, but how they had a plan using owls, falcons, and these white plastic tube like protection sheets on the grapevines. This was surprising to us all as we didn't know Liam and his brother Sean were thinking of other wineries being part of their business. While they owned 49% of Stonefruit Canyon, they seemed like they were fully focused on it. They explained how they're only partial owners and want something that's truly theirs. The hope they had for these new vines and the land in general was palpable. They were dreamers from the start, and were about to run their next winery. That was pretty impressive to me, but I still didn't understand what falcons and owls would do for the land. I still had a few things left to learn about wine it seems. So, I asked about it on the bus when there was a lull in the buzzy ride. Liam explained that there's people out there who train falcons to fly over a certain area, like the vineyard, the winery's grapevine land. They patrol, aka fly over, the area and essentially scare mice and rats from living there. These people were called Falconers and made a living doing this. That is, after the years of training and bonding with their birds of prey. I learned that vines don't want to be controlled, no matter how much time you train them, but sometimes nature can take over and play with the land to help control pests on it. As a yogi, I thought of this a Reiki for the vineyard. If neither of those references resonate, then think of it as a sibling backseat game of 'I'm not touching you" where you pester your siblings with the motions of tickling hands, but without actually laying a finger.

I like this idea of working with what you've been given, and gently changing things for the better like how the land was being worked into their new vineyard. This is very much what I was doing internally too, cultivating change. Because of this, I felt a kindred spirit with them. However, on the rest of the bus ride, awkwardness ensued when Tyler turned to me and said, "Your outfit matches your water bottle, is that like...your thing?" I thought to myself, *My thing? Do people really make "a thing" of matching their bottle's color to their outfits?* I looked at the lavender peasant-style dress from Target that I was wearing and my lilac-colored water bottle. I looked at him quizzically. "Not really," I replied and followed up with, "I just like wearing all types of color and things are bound to match eventually."

There's so much personality behind the brands of Paso. This team building event was designed to be our day though, and we were getting served something different than expected. We went to our third stop, a winery that was concrete everywhere, very Millennial Grey. It was cold inside too, being February, and they had dried flowers on each table we were to sit at. Being into flowers myself, I noticed these and thought the dried state of them matched the cold feeling of the tasting room. After being there a few moments, the owners came out to meet us. They were also the winemakers and essentially handled everything from wine club to marketing and bottle label design too. They were tall, lanky, artsy types that looked straight out of Topanga Canyon. They had big city prices too. Their advice for us was ironic as they said, "Wine is always living. It's never static. As the grape grows it never really stops. Even when it's in the bottle the wine continues to change and develop." Ironic in that their place wasn't vibrant and didn't feel full of life, but I appreciated the concept nonetheless. Wine is a lifestyle. The lifestyle of wine people and places all come together to make a great wine. I wondered how the Urban Hippy vibes from these winemakers would pair with the cement feeling of their facility. I felt skeptical about the success they would reap, and it made me appreciate the homey, welcoming nature of Stonefruit Canyon.

The female half of the duo at that winery said being a server in this industry is unique, she said, "Cocktails rely on the precise mixture of this and that, as does wine. A cocktail relies on the shape of the glass to tantalize the eyes, nose with its scent and taste buds with its flavor, as does wine. A bar tender, or mixologist, and someone working in the wine industry as a wine educator both rely on their skills pouring liquid into said glass." The male partner added in, "They both rely on their charm and showmanship when serving. The person enjoying the beverage is savoring the crafted experience that passes hands from grower, distiller, blender, bottler, labeler, packager, distributer, seller, opener, mixer, and server and so forth." I took it in and thought to myself, *Okay so that's something I learned from this visit*. But he went and made it awkward again, when he mentioned that in wine we don't have to worry about shaking a cocktail under the bar, and having it look like we're doing something else down there. Devin and Josh immediately urst out in laughter. They did the hand movement he was talking about. Doing it above the table they were seated at looked like a regular bartender shaking a cocktail shaker. When they did that same movement under the table and I couldn't see their hands completely, just the motion from their forearm, I knew something was up. This is when Ambrose's smile cracked into a boyish giggle. Josh winked right at Devin and Ambrose, who was sitting next to me. I thought to myself, *Uumm, did they just make a masturbation joke? Yes, yes, I think he did. Yuck.* I saw the boys make this connection and it was similar to the connection Betty and I had over her purse sandwich. It was camaraderie. It was bonding. It felt good to be part of the staff, and I wondered if our bosses knew the team-building aspect occurred a bit differently than expected. Our final stop led us to a where there was finally food prepared for us. This place has mastered flatbreads, sandwiches, and my favorite- the gourmet mac and cheese. I had been here before, but everything tasted even better on this day knowing I wasn't eating alone, but with friends.

"Penicillin cures, but wine makes people happy."
Alexander Fleming

REGION

O n the bus home towards the tasting room, Henry was talking to our coworker Devin about wine. He said, "Well ya' know how wine represents one particular region. Well, sometimes, in a blend, there's different types of wine but there's the one uniting fact that they are all from the same region." Devin thought about what Henry said, and added, "Like how a pinot noir is mixed with a chardonnay and they may have grown on different plots of land across the street from each other, but they are from the same place?" I thought these two were geeking out about wine, and I just felt like staring out the open window, hoping to not get car sick. An erudite, Devin had proven himself to be an insufferable know-it-all, but he was often right at least. The rutted dirt roads in Paso got me thinking about this further as I sat in silence waiting for the bus to take us back to the tasting room we started at. I also strived to be in my own head and didn't want to overhear too much from others' conversation. I was in deep thought trying to focus on the horizon, a trick I used to avoid getting car sick.

I was daydreaming and noticed what Henry said about wine vastly differs from cocktails which combine ingredients from all over the world. This is what separates mixed drinks from wine. A mixed drink, also called a cocktail, mixes something unique, say, a sweet potato liqueur from Atwater California into a shaker with something from far lands like Russia. This is how they differ. The origins of the liquids are vastly different. It seemed the meditative rolling hills on the Templeton Gap AVA brought

TASTING ROOM CONFIDENTIAL

inspiration to me as I hoped they would today. I had connected what Henry meant earlier and I understood that when different things are blended together, they're a nice alternative to when things are always the same.

This observation left me feeling relieved and happy because it seemed the personal development aspect of this day was indeed successful. I had in fact, learned more about my coworkers, Paso, and myself. Now, I may have just been dreaming of something else to drink other than the tiny water bottle Tammy gave us, or snooty wine, but I was thankful for where the rocky day had brought me. While I was feeling disappointed that we hadn't gone to any places I would choose to return to on my days off, I did have a little bit of fun. Plus, I was taking in Betty's advice that it was a good practice to only visit three wineries a day.

After work, I felt peer pressure to hang out with my coworkers, but I had fatigued my extroverted side today and wanted to go home to my son. Just like I spent my days off with my son, I wanted to spend my evenings with him too. He truly was he was the best company. We loved building LEGO together and playing dress up in our backyard. I was happy to clock out of work for the day to play with him. Betty liked to drink but admitted, "A few quality experiences are preferable to numerous and unmemorable pours that'll end up swirling together in your head." I felt my son's company was the highest quality there was.

NIGHT OUT

Preferring nights in with my son over nights out with friends, I only said yes one time when Josh was organizing a get together after work. He hoped we'd all join him for happy hour at a steakhouse in downtown Paso. He had been bugging us about it at work for weeks and promised us this delicious appetizer with beef tips covered in a cilantro cream sauce over French fries was worth it. He pitched it to Betty saying there were low priced drinks. She laughed at him, and said, "Josh I don't pay for drinks when I go out. I only paid for *these* before I go out!" As she pointed to her high heels which she was dangling from her hands. She wore high heels as she was dressed as the girl on the Stonefruit Canyon Malbec bottle for Halloween and had accidentally left the heels at the tasting room. She had taken them off when she tired of the sores they were causing on her toes. Taking them home today, she had them in hand when he invited us all out again. Josh shook his head in the exasperated sort of way men did when women did womanly things they don't exactly understand their attraction to. Josh continued his pitch and explained that he knew the waitress who would be working the night we went there and she would "hook it up." This generous invitation was extended to Riley, Betty, Ambrose, and myself. Because it's between home and the tasting room so it's easy to see how he would go often after work.

When I got there, I noticed the second reason he'd likely go there a lot. The beautiful blonde working at the bar. Yes, she was undeniably beautiful, but also tough in the way women have to be when they work happy hour shifts at bars. She definitely looked like she could talk back to those who deserved it. I was first to arrive, which isn't something new for me. Even though I'd moved here from Los Angeles a decade ago, I still overestimated how long everything took to get to because of traffic. Except, there was no traffic here, so I was always early. I usually kept a book in my car for moments like this. When it was only minutes before our 6pm meet up time, I walked into the restaurant, and upstairs. We met up in the bar on second floor just as he described, and started looking over the menu. I saw the beef and fries dish he'd recommended but I ended up ordering something healthy, like I was taught a girl should do in public. Josh ordered a pilsner beer, and joked, "It takes a lot of beer to make good wine." He was pretty funny most of the time, I thought. I ordered a seven and seven cocktail as it was the most fun cocktail to say, and I enjoyed that it was sweet, but not too sweet.

We chatted after ordering our first round of appetizers. Our first plate of food came and no other coworkers had strolled in. I was sure Betty would come; she doesn't cook at home. I understood Riley probably had a Skype date with her girlfriend, and Ambrose probably lit a blunt right when he got clocked out after work and forgot he was supposed to join us. I was sipping on my cocktail and as I drank and I noticed the ice cubes looked the icebergs floating in a tan and sandy ocean, I realized we'd been there a while. The ice had watered down the whiskey. Our second appetizer came; garlic fries this time. We continued to chat. We had been here long enough for my drink to be nearly finished. There were just a few fries left on the plate, and we were still alone. Josh asked about my relationship and wanted to know how long I'd been married. I confided that I wasn't actually married to my son's dad. Looking puzzled, he asked quizzically, "But you wear a ring?" I sighed a big sigh, and felt comfortable telling him the truth. I shared that it was an engagement ring, and that I really wanted it to mean more than it did.

I always knew I'd be a mom one day. We stopped paying attention one afternoon in September and got pregnant. But that wasn't in his 5-Year Business Plan, so we compromised and made a contract. He would pay rent and give me a small allowance to buy household things with, and in turn I would take care of my baby, do dishes and laundry, and tidying. I also managed the paperwork for health insurance, posted to our family blog that grandparents read daily, and signed up for and took my son to enrichment programs.

I shared how I cried myself to sleep many nights. This was not the life I imagined. This was not the family I imagined. I felt like a single mother with a roommate. I felt so alone, like a fraud. Family is supposed to be home, not a place. I wanted to make a home with my son and his dad, but he didn't want to get married. The best he could do was give me this ring he proudly purchased in Oregon without sales tax. As I talked more, I felt rushed as I felt unsure and a bit embarrassed. I told Josh how I had forgotten some of the things that happened with him, and that honestly, how I would like to keep it that way. Josh said, "It's okay Jenn, you can tell me." He felt genuine. I looked around and noticed we were still the only ones there. I shared how I wanted marriage and was willing to go off the beaten path for it. When my persistence to marry would get my son's father annoyed, he gave me an excuse. I was good at circumventing the excuses. I was a wedded bliss barrier basher. I bashed all the barriers that he'd find. He said weddings cost too much, so I got creative. I had just won an Instagram contest for a free night's stay at a beautiful coastal hotel. I had asked my stylist friend to do my hair, and she said yes. I booked a Benefit brand makeover at ULTA so my makeup was pretty, and free. I booked a new photographer who hoped to build a wedding portfolio, so she gave us a screaming great deal for an hour of her time. I wore a dress I already owned, and bought a little cake from Madonna Inn. We even had childcare covered. I brought our son to my folks' house so they would watch him for us while we went to the beach. He said he didn't want to involve the government with marriage licenses and the like. So, I had scheduled for us to just make promises to love each other. I explained my plans. We could be alone on the beach at sunset, and promise our commitment to one another. This would be free, from government marriage licenses and free from officiant fees. I hoped to make him happy, and at the same time make myself feel good inside, and legitimize our son. This all would feel like we had made a promise to each other, and it would have sufficed. I would feel my son wasn't from a roommate or even a boyfriend and girlfriend relationship, but from a real married couple. On that day, were running behind schedule, and my son's dad needed a snack before the photoshoot. So, instead of using the pre-picture time for beachside promises, he said he was really hungry, so we got McDonalds drive thru and sat in the car. At least we got to view the ocean at twilight, but I didn't get the dreamy seaside promises. I didn't get a kiss at sunset. Basically, I didn't get what we agreed to, or what my ring symbolized. But I didn't want to cry and ruin my makeup, or worse, give him a real reason to not marry me if I was being a naggy "wife," so I played it cool. After his burgers, we did our fake wedding photoshoot, ate carrot cake, and fell asleep in the lavish hotel room.

Josh was right, there was more to that story, when he asked said, "Wow, and then what happened?" I chuckled, sensing he could handle a bit more of my dirty laundry. I continued on explaining that I was well-practiced at being persistent, and resourceful. From the outside it looked like I had gotten what I wanted, so I convinced myself that pictures and a ring was enough. When we got the photos back from the photographer, they were beautiful. I wanted to share them with family on the family blog that I ran. I wanted to shout it from seaside cliffs, "We're married! We're a real family!" but he advised me that it was more appropriate to wait until the family visited our home and saw the pictures hanging in the hallway for themselves. Now, I wasn't sure how this would work because many family lives far away in Oregon and the San Francisco Bay Area and rarely travelled to visit us, but I was willing to play along.

It felt good to tell Josh the whole truth that no one else knew. Josh's second beer was nearly finished when I looked over at it. There were just a few white bubbles of foam left on about an inch of its amber color. He sat back in his chair, held up his glass and said, "Damn girl, you've certainly gone through a lot! Cheers to you...a single badass mom!" I held up my now ice water and said "Cheers!" with him. Just then I felt my phone buzz in my back pocket. It was nearing 8PM. Talking and enjoying ourselves made time slip on by. I had told my son's dad I was going out with coworkers after we closed the tasting room, and would be back at 8 to get our son to bed. I worried that the movie version of this scene had my son's dad storm into the bar wondering why we were there alone. I felt so guilty but had done nothing wrong. Sharing the truth was freeing, but also revealing and felt wrong. I felt like my decision to finally go out and be social would bite me in the ass. I spiraled with my worries, and only came out of it when the bartender asked if she could get me another drink. She handed me a menu with her question, and I handed it to Josh. Our hands brushed. Had he felt my hand or did he think it was the padfolio thing the happy hour menu was in? I fretted. I looked at the bartender, and quickly said, "Oh, no. No thank you. I have to go soon." I replied like Cinderella realizing it was nearly midnight. I wouldn't exactly turn into a pumpkin tonight for it was only 7:45, and the tasting room *closed* closed, like we got it all cleaned and prepped for tomorrow around 6, so I wasn't even out too late. Josh and I had been chatting for nearly two hours though. Despite this logic, I was dreading my mistake to let time slip by even more when I heard my own worried feelings. *This felt very much like a date* I thought again. Had Josh even told our coworkers about today's meet up, or did he just tell me they were invited too? Was my crush on him still hidden or was there any possibility he had one on me as well? Definitely not after what I just blurted out to him. There was so much more I could have shared, and so much I was curious about. For now, what I did know is that I had to get out of there. I handed Josh a folded $20 bill as well as a crinkly $10 bill I received as a tip during today's shift, in effort to pay my half of the bill. Josh refused. This should have felt nice, but it worried me further. With him paying for me, that definitely felt like a date move. I was so confused. He did call me a badass single mom, so at least I had that going for me.

WILD NOSES RUN FREE

Being in a rural location, sometimes things go wrong due to the nature around us. Nature can be wild, and have some real impacts. Like at Stonefruit Cellars the water well was drying up and not working because the pump was broken. The negative to this is far beyond not having lots of water to aid in plant growth, but it also caused a bad smell outside near the well. On these stinky smelly bad well days, I learned that I should not do a tour of the vines out back. No tour of beauty for favorite customers and not even a bad tour for those rude customers. It's far too unpleasant to be out there smelling it ourselves. Plus, it's important to keep your karma healthy. Being a "supertaster" goes with being a "supersmeller" and on those broken pump days, I wish that on no one. Because no matter the weather, we are selling class in a glass. We are selling comfort, connection, and flavor in these sips. We are selling the lifestyle of this old school house in reverence for the countryside. Speaking of countryside happenings, if we left Georgia's leftover snack from the night before on the patio table, you would not have a good experience. Just one little thing can ruin it and we all work hard to make sure that the things we can control are kept within our control. You see, as wild as this experience feels as it's very outdoorsy and very nature, very wild and free. It is still a manicured experience. We are giving you the experience that we want you to have to have your best experience on that day and because of this no tasting will be the same. Just like how the wine will feel different in the hands of a different guest.

To get a break from all this responsibility we distract ourselves with more responsibility. Employees retreat to the back of the house, in the kitchen where we all hang out as our respite between customers. On the countertops, there's a constant array of used wine glasses with a little bit of wine stating the bottom. Oh, and so many towels, too. Half the dish towels that we need to polish the glasses are wet hanging to dry and the other half are holey or hanging to dry from the day before. They're never actually folded in the drawer that's labeled "towels" as they're the most used item in the kitchen area. In the employee fridge, are our employee lunches that are consumed quickly as the timer is watching us.

SWEET WORDS

One day we had a reservation for a group of eight people. Before they came, we made sure we had a table outside for them and enough clean glasses. We also organized who would pour for them. Well, it was me. So, when the reservation time arrived, we started looking in the parking lot for the party to arrive. We were looking for two vehicles or maybe even a party bus that was rented with the purpose of hauling people from winery to winery safely all day. When they finally arrived 15 or so minutes late, it was in fact a large vehicle that probably was quite packed even so, as when they came out of the car, it was amazing they all fit. As they approached the tasting room, they paused to see the big chair, as all are apt to do. When they came inside, I was the one to verbally greet them. They looked around and one asked where the bathroom was. I pointed to the bathroom at the end of the bar, and said, "Just there around the corner!" with a smile. One of their group asked me to only pour them the sweet wines today, as they wanted to make Grandma happy. Knowing our wines tend to be dry in taste on the palate, I said, "Humm, I am sad to say that we don't really have sweet wines here at Stonefruit Canyon. We certainly have a Port wine that I could offer, so I showed them that bottle and picked a glass for the man who was at my counter when I returned from getting the bottle. I had been told that the port wine has its label made before the law passed that "port" had to come from Portugal, and our winery was grandfathered in, so we can have that label on this sweet wine, and I tell him this, to which I got no reply from him. I poured a little bit and explained, that "The wine is sweet on the palate, and strong in nature as it's fortified with brandy. Fortified means made stronger with alcohol, and that our winery used brandy — which also comes from grapes. With its higher alcohol by volume, or ABV for short, it's made to last longer since the high alcohol helps to make the wine not go bad even after the bottle is opened." I tell him our particular winery makes the Port in a way called Solera Style which is nonvintage, meaning that it's wine and brandy from different years' harvests. By combining zinfandel wine to the port year after year, there's elements in the bottle that are 30 years old and some that are just one. Since it's stronger ABV, I poured the gentleman a small sip for him to get a sense of the drink before committing to ordering it for his entire party, including Grandma, as he was intending to do as they only wanted sweet wines. So, when I pour the port, he looks at me like I am being stingy. I use my canned reply when this happens, "Try it before you think you want more." And he does. Another woman re-approaches the bar, and rests her large bedazzled, hobo style bag on the bar. She says, "I pick this winery for sweet wine. What they have? I try." And he turns to her and speaks Spanish. She's upset, and I wish I had taken Spanish in high school instead of the German and French classes I took instead. Yearning to help and do anything I could, I get another glass from behind the bar and place it in front of her. I pour a little bit of the port and she says "More," and gives me eye contact, so I pour more in her glass. She smells and drinks it, and says to me, "It good."

He asks to buy a bottle, and I reach for one from behind the bar. I set it on the bar, and his deep brown eyes get even bigger. He says, "That it?" and more of his family members approach the bar after browsing the kitschy merchandise for sale in the tasting room. I inform him that "Yes, the port comes in a bottle like this," and that's in fact, the same size bottle I was pouring from so I line the two up.

He wants to know why it's smaller than the wine bottles, and I say that because it's higher ABV, it's a smaller bottle. He is upset, and said with a tsk, "Why I buy big bottle with handle at liquor store, but small bottle here?" I reply, "Tradition," and ring him up for the $28 and ask if he would like me to open the bottle to enjoy it here or if he prefers that I package it to go. He says, "I drink here," and I figure that he needed two glasses by the two fingers he held up when he said that. I use my wine bottle opener, officially called a wine key, and open the bottle. I stick the cork slightly back in the bottle, and give him a paper bag with a handle on it and say it's for the rest of the bottle so he can transport it home discretely.

Upon seeing the handle on the bag, I giggle to myself — he indeed "get a handle" for his bottle today, but he definitely had the last laugh because what he did next came as a total surprise to me. He took the cork off the just-opened bottle and poured half in his glass and half in the other glass and then slid the empty bottle back to me. Shocked is the only word to describe me in that moment. Then utter desperate hope that he, or the woman that imbibed, were not the ones driving the car for their party. I was also left wondering when Grandma would get her taste, as hadn't they come specifically for her? Boggled. Utterly boggled yet again.

KLEPTO

In between customers, I was talking to Josh about the upcoming Wine Club party. I said, "I feel like at these winery parties people always want something. Anything. Get a little wine in them, and they all turn into kleptos. Especially flowers because they think it won't be reused at the winery."

Lots of things go missing during large events, and sometimes things show up as well. Like when we're closing the tasting room and find something while carrying out its many procedures. I guessed Karma balanced out sometimes when you lost something you may find something later on too. Preparing for events was Betty and Josh's expertise as they wanted to prepare for the following day. In addition to the kitchen, there's the bar that needs to be wiped down, the windows to be locked, and all this in efforts to be set for our tasting room's next customers. We also have to add a layer of argon gas to the top of the wine in the bottles. This stops air from touching the wine, and making it taste different. I learned from Josh that it's an "inert gas" meaning it doesn't harm humans. Plus, it looks pretty badass to have a huge five-foot argon tank at the tasting room bar.

At events the tasting room and outside picnic tables often had centerpieces, which were often the things that were taken, despite their inconvenience. This happened with the succulent cactus arrangements at Stonefruit Canyon that were just as often stuffed in purses as the wine glasses. A purse fill of cactus' — I couldn't image that being fun to empty out of your purse when you get home. Imagine trying to find your keys. People boggled me sometimes.

The next Wednesday at my book club, my friend tells me her mom nabs glasses when they go out wine tasting. "I feel so bad. I have asked to buy them but the tasting people usually tell her to go ahead. But I haven't gone out tasting with her in forever because it's embarrassing," my friend says. I retorted, realizing I was the resident wine expert in the club, "Wine tasting is supposed to be classy, come on people!" and they all chuckle. Knowing that a little wine and sunshine definitely made people act different. Keeping the glasses from a tasting event, is a holdover from the 90's when all wineries gave glasses as a souvenir with the tasting. It was a great tradition but now the wineries are paying for it, because old-school wine people haven't updated their kleptomaniac nature, erm, I mean souvenir-taking, habits. "I mean, it really would be nice to never wash glasses if they took the dirty glasses with them," I said. Josh replied, "But nowadays the glasses are way nicer since they aren't meant to be given away." The glass' shape has an effect on the nose of the wine, as it can allow more oxygen touch the liquid, it can directly make or break the wine. So, the winery had intentionally decided to buy the best glasses available in efforts to enhance their already delicious wine. Polishing glasses later that day, he added, "The couple freebie glasses I have at home are the basic, small, boring shape glasses that I bust out if people are going to be drunk and I don't care if they break." He trails off when he heard the office telephone rang. Returning from answering the call from a potential customer asking if we serve lunch at the winery, he didn't miss a beat in our conversation, "They have way nicer glasses at most places now, and I do think it can make a difference in the wine's flavor, but it's more of an ambiance setter for me. I love the feel of good wine glass. None of this stemless trend. I like these Stoltze brand ones here, but there's also Riedel…those are nice." Tucking this info aside for the moment, I prep my smile to greet my first customer duo of the day.

After work tonight there's one of the sporadically scheduled, Wine Industry Nights. This is a time when wineries stay open past the typical tasting room hours of 10-5pm, and invite other wine professionals over to try their wine. It's basically a time to socialize and party. Since working in the industry means you generally love wine, but are too busy to wine taste at other locations, staying open during a Wine Industry Night is a kind way to share and show off your offerings to those in the know. Ever on the romantic prowl, Betty and Josh often attended these and reported back to me the next day, saying, "You should come with us next time, Jenn, it'd be great!"

"Hey, why don't we get one hosted here?" I ask, knowing the winery owner's generous nature definitely makes that a possibility. Betty said, "Well because most people in the industry began their career here first, so they've had our wines before. Wine Industry Night are about trying something new." I thought about what Betty said, and wondered where the industry would take me. Would I go to different winery sometime? Would I run into these coworkers again? I imagined it being like a reunion of sorts, and didn't want to work without these particular humans at a winery ever again. I also felt especially grateful that Stonefruit Cellars was welcoming to newbies. They really embodied the teaching aspect that their old schoolhouse vibes imply.

DANDELION

It's not where you work but who you work with that makes it tolerable. Even the most daunting of jobs gets better with the help of coworkers. Henry embodied the perfect tasting room wine educator at a family-run place like Stonefruit Canyon. He shelved his ego as to not be off-putting. Sure, he was a published author and former professor, but when it comes to spewing comedy or wine facts, he was very humble.

The big chair out front of the tasting room worked like a magnet to attract customers to our parking lot. They wanted a photo of themselves in the big chair. It dwarfed customers, making the people feel so small. It was so big in fact that people they had to jump into it to sit and pose for a photo. Whenever Henry saw this, he would tell his joke, "Oh look, the alcohol really did stunt your growth!" I felt that only he could get away with saying a joke like that.

I thought of Henry as a dandelion flower. Many would point to him as a weed, but he had medicinal properties with his therapeutic demeanor and helped bring people, like pollinators, to the garden of our tasting room., Many customers were such a fan of Henry, the perennial dandelion, that they returned again and again and hoped he would be the one pouring for them.

ICE

I was researching wine on my own by now and had read the bestselling Wine Folly book like it was the Bible. I also watched older movies like Bottle Shock and favorite, Sideways, I found myself daydreaming about wine. Fresh with the idea of wine being from a single place and cocktails being combined from elements all over the world, I happened to go to a Paso favorite for dinner, Magical Gastronomy. It's a restaurant on The Square in downtown Paso. Sitting at the bar, the bartender told me they have one of the most expensive water filtration systems in the county. Coming to the cost of $10,000, "It's a high investment just to make sure the ice is clear." I looked at my cocktail and thought it did look particularly clear now that you say it, but I wouldn't have noticed had you not said anything. It felt nice to be at a bar, but on the drinking side of it. The bartenders at Magical Gastronomy take the lead from the restaurant's investment a bit further and temper the ice, which is a process to make sure the doesn't crack in your glass. If you're into that sort of thing, or, adversely not into ice with cracks in it, then the cocktails at Magical Gastronomy are for you. All this had me learning of the visual experience and how it is part of the success of the cocktail. I was glad I didn't have to learn mixology techniques at Stonefruit Canyon, but there certainly were so many varietals to learn about and what kind of food to pair with wine, and the temperature it should be enjoyed at. It was once said that, "The romance in wine is definitely in drinking it. It's a lot of hard work to make it." I related to the hard work. The combination of mixing things old and new reminded me that there were different paths to success, and how important my high threshold for failure was. I was learning that the most questionable choices I've ever made were a direct result of survival mode and low self-esteem. This restaurant invested so much money to make ice more like the ice of your dreams. I felt certain I had more value than ice did. My value is inherent and isn't dependent on a machine process. When I walked into the tasting room, I knew I belonged.

After thinking about my experience at the restaurant, I was reminded of the Forbes hospitality training I went to with Tammy. I noticed how presentation is so important to both industries — wine and restaurant. I also noticed something mind boggling that changed the way I look at drinks. Wine is blended with grapes from the same vineyard or region, where as cocktails are blended together with things from all offer the world. Thinking further, I noticed there's a notion in wine that "what grows together, goes together" meaning that food is distinguished regionally and different foods are from different areas. This is often seen in pizzas, hot dog styles, and sandwiches. Similarly, wine is different from different regions. Some believe the rule of thumb says that wine can be best paired with food from the same region, and this was so contrary to that philosophy. Where some would insist on earthy pinot noir which thrives in cold climate, as do mushrooms, is enough to make them a match made in heaven, cocktails didn't need to be matched to the food as much. And when you do pair food with cocktails, you're not limited by what it's near but rather people's preferences and ability to procure things from around the world.

THE TIPPING POINT

When I began working at Stonefruit Canyon in springtime, it was strictly, "no tips," meaning that there wasn't an option on the computer screen when customers bought something in the tasting room using their cards. Cash tips were allowed to be accepted, but in reality, people don't carry much cash with them anymore, so even though cash tips could be discreetly given to us, they were few and far between. And because very few customers saw others tipping cash, they didn't tip either. It was contagious. However, this radically changed as coworkers like Betty brought up the facts to management. Fact one being that it doesn't cost the company any money and that people would tip if they wanted to. Fact two, this would help reduce employee turnover. People noticed we were not getting tips and since it has become such an industry standard, people were leaving the winery after short stints. The best and worst comes out of all those who call this place home, and those who call this their vacation destination, when money and alcohol mix. Phrases that accompany the iPad's spin to the customer to finish the transaction leave much to the imagination. In the service sector, I've had servers say things like, "Oh the iPad is just going to ask you a few questions," as if they don't know that's the tip screen when they hand it to you. This is the most awkward of sentences, really. We're in this position of educator and knowledgeable about the winery and wines but saying this makes us look like the newbie who doesn't know what's happening. There's also the popular, "Please follow the prompts on the screen," which is ugly too as it makes it seem like we're not used to the transaction process. As if we've never made a purchase in our life. The transaction is uncomfortable for all parties. I have found that the most effective and mutually rewarding practice was to call out the oddity, and mention what it means. I eventually found my own way of doing this with the phrase "Tips are always appreciated but never expected." This helps people who haven't been responsible for holding an iPad in a restaurant setting, and those who were new to this version of self-checkout which was trending in tasting rooms. As people's generosity towards the service sector grew, the notion of tipping sometimes gob smacked the face of everyone paying with a credit card. As credit card payments made computer interfaces include a point of sale also a point of tipping, adding on 10%, 15%, or 20% became a button push versus having cash on hand.

There's a phrase, "Empty pockets, big smiles," which means that if people pay for an experience, they're more likely to see that situation as fun and worthwhile to them. While people like the choice and decision-making experience to analyze the tipping, after some time in the industry, I have noticed there's a generational divide with this when it comes to tipping after receiving a stellar service. Younger people see it as an obligation and the older generations see the social contract as a choice. Regardless of generation and circumstance, it's about service. That's because good customer service equals happiness, and happiness equals bigger tips. I noticed that tipping was different around the holidays, which proved to me that tipping is emotional. Also regulating customers to give tips, is the tech involved. The app-based payment system, with the suggested tip amounts, makes you more likely to do it. These screens are quite a sticky situation. It may feel like emotional blackmail based on inherent social awkwardness.

As tipping screens are now the norm when paying with a credit card, in 2019 and in prior years, tipping at Stonefruit

Canyon wasn't really allowed. Seen as taboo, and something for others, the policy at the winery was that if someone left a cash tip, it was yours to keep, but if they wanted to add it to the credit card transaction, they couldn't. This policy paired with people's tendency to carry less cash around made for many awkward a moment when the customer wants to tip like when I had a customer who said, "Oh, no. I want to add a tip for you on my tab, but I don't see that option. Did I miss something?" as they hand the iPad back to me. "No, it's actually not on there. You didn't miss anything. We can't accept tips on the credit card transaction like other places." Over and over again, people leave feeling bad they couldn't thank us, and feel regretful they don't carry cash. Even with reassuring that, "It's totally fine, we're okay," having folks leave with regret is not really a feeling that's in the best interest of the company. Having people leave satisfied about their experience, and able to express it by tipping staff, is not only preferred by everyone, but also probably better for business.

There's an unspoken can of worms of sexual harassment around tipping pretty/attractive people. I experimented one day with my outfit choice mimicking what I saw waitresses wear at bars before. I wore a low-cut spaghetti strap tank top that showed cleavage. I set this outfit out the night before and prepared it as pure research wanting to compare the tips I received that day versus a day with a solid color winery-branded t-shirt. The results were as expected in a visually-influenced society. In the tank top my tips were $68 for the six-hour shift, whereas when I wore the t-shirt, they were added up to be $42. I don't think this was coincidental. Correlation between a 30% increase in tips when I showed some skin versus modest dress is notable and proof that presenting yourself as on-display, so to speak, is unfair, but absolutely something that happens in this type of environment. I wish it wasn't true, and I also wish I could do my makeup a certain way to run the experiment again and make it about facial beauty instead of cleavage. I am sure this is true of men too, as Josh and Devin were making more money in tips than Henry was.

Workers become dependent on tips, and worked harder to earn more. Like the Forbes training taught us — the service industry is one of the few industries where you choose how much money you make as you can earn more by providing remarkable experiences for your guests.

When thinking about the fact that my appearance affected how people tipped me, thus proving their thankfulness and admiration of me, I started to wonder if this really relates to wine bottle labels too. Do pretty labels sell for higher rates than more plain bottles? Does the font on the label matter? Does the wax capped bottle sell for more than a foil cap or exposed cork bottle? Ultimately, I wondered who was in charge of these design choices and what research goes beyond it. I was also reminded of that song, with the lyric of, "There may be a little dust on the bottle, but don't let that fool you about what's inside." And I wondered if the singer was being literal and speaking about dust on the wine bottles, or if he meant it metaphorically about people as we age.

In the tasting room, when I would ring someone up for their wine purchase, give them a smile, and say my usual, "Tips are always appreciated, but never expected," I was being very honest. Plus, it says thank you before even being given anything. Plus, our customer service and knowledge didn't end as soon as we ring someone up. This also nods to the inherent meaning of tips — letting people thank others for exceptional service. Lastly, it ends the transaction with a positive emotion. I loved this so much and translated it to myself. My value is inherent and not something that could be taken from me. I knew my value doesn't depend on which tip button people press, although people liked to judge my value. Pay period after pay period, Tammy noticed a trend in people's tips and noticed I was the winery's highest tip earner. Perhaps it was this simple act of acknowledging, and being thankful, that helped ensure this position. When our inherent belief is that we are already worthy just as we are, we begin making choices that actually honor our needs, values, and wellbeing. I began to act based on my needs, not just the fear of not being enough.

CALIFORNIA TIP

There's more to California than great wine. In fact, many people love to come here for our liberal laws about marijuana. There were some regulations here about how much and from where, but generally marijuana isn't taboo like stories from straightlaced Boomers make it seem. One Sunday, while working in the tasting room, I learned that people fly into the area, landing at our airport in San Luis Obispo (SBP), to add some of that California green herb to their recreational travel plans. I learned about this way of enjoying Paso after the fact though.

In hindsight it was a very normal experience pouring for this couple. They were curious, but didn't want to talk about what paired with the wine when drinking it at home as they said their bags were full and they didn't want to ship wine home, so they were only drinking wine that day and had no intention of buying bottles. This was absolutely fine with me, and I actually appreciated their upfront approach to getting the most out of their vacation. Not everyone is so honest with their intention to get some alcohol in their system and move on to the next winery. Winery hopping is similar to bar hopping, and to the under 21, can compare it to changing the radio station from one station to another — getting your fix one song, or glass of wine, at a time.

The couple clarified their safety in this binge practice and told me that they had a driver picking them up soon, and that they were heading to the airport to fly home to Texas. I asked how their trip was and what other wineries they visited and if they had any favorite restaurants or shops. They must have answered me because it was a pleasant conversation, but their question back to me stopped me in my tracks and boggled my brain so much I was dumbfounded. You see, they asked me if they could give me a different kind of tip, as the wife held up a plastic tube. Inside I was pretty sure it was a legit hand-rolled marijuana cigarette. A blunt. It was in a little plastic tube that reminded me of high school science class so I had to really look at it again to understand what they were asking me. I must have looked as confused as I felt, as the man added, "That is, if you would enjoy something like this? We'd hate for it to go to waste because we can't bring it back home to Texas with us. TSA wouldn't like that one bit. But would you?"

I played it cool, not wanting to reject a tip and said "Yes, that would be lovely. Thank you." And took the iPad back from them after they signed for their tasting fees, and also took the unique tip from them. I chuckled and said, "That's the most California tip ever," to which they told me "It's from a local shop which has great stuff."

I examined the tube and saw the words "Indoor. Exotic. THC hybrid. Pre-roll." *Alright, well that's unique*, I thought to myself. I would remember this work experience for quite some time, but I had a new question for myself — what to do with it? I shyly slipped it in my front left pocket and walked back into the tasting room. I went to the kitchen to add their glasses to the dishwasher and saw Josh drinking a Red Bull. I felt comfortable telling him, so I leaned in close to him, and explained to him, "I got a very unique tip — they gave me this," as I held out my hand. His big eyes lit up, and said, "No way Jenn! That's rad!" He paused, "But what are you going to do with it?" I told him maybe my son's dad would like it, as he was into that sort of stuff. After work that day I was excited about this very different thing I would be bringing home. It certainly was different than the bottles of old wine we couldn't pour for our customers anymore. I was proud of the blunt at this point, as I had earned this gift, this memory, and this wild story from work. When I got home, I went to my son's dad's office and stood in the doorway. "I got an interesting tip today," I said as I gave it to him. He nonchalantly examined it, and asked whether it was Indica or Sativa, as he wanted to "know what he was getting into." I told him I didn't know, but assured him that my customers said it was from a good local place. He said, "That's cool," and he sat back at his desk and added it to his stash, while saying "Thanks."

AMERICANA

O nce when pouring for two customers, I said Stonefruit Canyon feels like living a Norman Rockwell painting. It's such a peaceful countryside vibe and bucolic setting. Much to my surprise, the older man I was pouring wine for leaned close over the bar, to speak closer to me and revealed that he was a fan of Rockwell too. He was with a younger woman who I assumed was his daughter who piped in, "You're a fan?" and the three of us exchanged a few moments of awe about the classic American art. The man leaned in towards me to speak again and said that when he was a little boy, he was featured in a Rockwell painting. Shocked, I asked, "Mind if you show me the painting on your phone?" It was frowned upon to have our phones in the tasting room, so I leaned over the bar and saw the photo. Thanks to the authentic photorealism of Rockwell's style, I could see the resemblance between the boy he was and the man he grew into. "That's a pretty incredible modeling gig of sorts!" I said, in amazement. The young woman said, "Plus, it's even more wild you even mentioned that painter right now, with him here. He's usually shy talking about that because it's when he was a boy and he didn't know the painter would be so popular nowadays." This felt like small-town Americana at its finest. Art resembled life. Well, at least in that Aristotelian moment.

ELECTRICITY

One day the tasting room experienced a power outage. It was fun at first, the music had stopped, yes, but that's all that we noticed. Our personal lunches would remain cold in the staff refrigerator for quite some time, and the rosé and white wines we were pouring would remain cold for at least an hour in the little fridge behind the bar. Oh, and the fact that the big stash of wine in the cellar didn't need to be refrigerated at all! But the reality of a power outage in a tasting room came quickly when someone needed to pay for their tasting experience and the wines they selected. Our iPads were not working with the wifi. There was no calculating the price of their totals, there was no 8.25% tax added in, and there was nothing calculated for us. Armed with smartphones, Josh, Ambrose, and I didn't hesitate to do the math manually on our phones. But then what — what would communicate to their credit card company?

Our manager Tammy came out from the back office with an idea. An archaic machine that was in its heyday before any of us had been born. This tool, a manual credit card imprinter and slider, was supposed to save the day. Tammy's face when she didn't get the exclaimed, "Yay," she'd expected when she brought out this day-saving device was memorable as all hell. We were all dumbfounded and needed her to show us how the thing was even supposed to work. Her dismay didn't end at the device usage, but also with our cluelessness at the paper that went along with it. Three copies of a receipt? What do the colors mean? Tammy could have felt surprised by the fact we didn't know what do, and maybe even a bit of "Wow, they're so young" feelings too. But no, what's unique about Tammy is that she was elated to be able to take us under her wing and do something to help for once. The tasting room ran without a manager for many months before she came, and we were all a bit used to the ins and outs of that. But actually, being needed meant the world to her. She was a happy and patient teacher showing us about how to place the credit card this certain way, and how to lay the redundant paper this certain way, and so forth.

THERE'S AN APP FOR THAT

A s part of my training, I learned the app that many tasting rooms use is called WineArrow. It is the cash register app, but for the back end of the tasting room, it also helps organize the daily sales, the wine club members, inventory, and keeps track of previous orders and upcoming wine club shipments. Basically, it's the tasting room organizer. The app is so busy and multifaceted handling all the business for the tasting rooms. It can be harnessed as a tool to help look up people's previous orders so employees can provide excellent customer service. We can look up what wine they buy the most of, and use that to offers suggestions and notices that the new vintage of that grape is being bottled soon, for example. It also let us employees see who is listed on the membership. This is handy if someone comes to pick up for your wine club allotment for you as they can request the wine on your behalf, and it's helpful in remembering people's names. For example, if the wine educator looks up member "Jason Chardonnay," for example, in the notes it may be listed "Wife Patricia" and the educator can help make the couple feel welcomed and remembered from visit to visit.

Knowing this little trick, I would often make fast friends and lots of tips with this trick. However, one day this backfired. A couple came to the tasting room and wanted to pick up their recent wine club allotment and do a taste and enjoy a picnic while they were in town. As this was a regular event, I went about my routine of looking up the couple's names in effort to give good customer service.

After establishing the rapport inside the tasting room, and learning his name to look up the account, I felt comfortable to say their name when delivering the wine to the picnic table. I placed one glass in front of Dan, and said his name, and while placing the other glass, I said "Here you go Helen." Dan's face developed a quick flush and a look of horror. He said, "Um, the account needs to be updated! That's my ex-wife's name and you need to meet my girlfriend, Charlotte." Oh my God, I messed up and learned that sometimes too much information can yield bad results. While the couple did seem to enjoy the scenery during their picnic, I guessed the alcohol was helping numb the feelings that Dan was just taking Charlotte to all the same places he'd taken his wife and the experience wasn't unique to her. I hoped they'd laugh about this later.

GREAT TIPPER

One weekend, Betty was working the bar with me and she was pouring for her customer, and a male of the pair asked for a larger pour than the standardized ounce size. I tuned in to hear this, as I was hoping to learn a clever way to reply if this ever happened to me. She handled it so cool; I was stunned. She said, "Well, it's our 2019, newly released, Pony River zinfandel wine. You haven't tried it yet. How do you know if you want more?"

Dang she's good! What a great way to defuse the situation, I thought. He smiled and sipped. Making eye contact with her again, he followed up with, "There. I like it. Can I have more?" and in a quieter whisper voice, he followed up with, "I'm a great tipper!"

Now, our bottles are not controlled like at bars where the management can control your pours of liquor with a regulator or something, so we technically can pour more. It doesn't seem fair to others though, and while we are motivated by money, there's something icky about these kinds of interactions. Betty, once again, the verbal chess player she is replied to him, "Well you have two more pours of our wine left in your tasting, so I can move you along to our cabernet sauvignon and petit verdot, if you'd like."

I knew I could learn a lot from her. I could use my wit to talk back in a nice way. This would get the tasting over with sooner, as he was finishing all his allotted tastes, and it wouldn't keep them lingering on the third taste as he tried to get more sips from that bottle. Betty knew how to stick to her guns, and be disarming all at once. Pure class.

GENERATIONAL DIVIDE

I overheard a conversation between a grandmother and her adult granddaughter. They're at the bar discussing what to order and who generally likes what. After looking over the menu, they look decided so I asked them if they're ready for me to take their order. The grandmother looks up from the menu, and gives me eye contact and said, "I'll have a glass of the rosé." She turns to her granddaughter and said, "And if I don't like it, you can have it deary."

"Well, I am not going to drink yours," the granddaughter replied to her.

"Why not?" the grandmother questioned.

"Because you might have diseases," the granddaughter replied. Burn. Total burn. She then said she'll just grab an energy drink from inside, but would like it in a wine glass too, so they can match. Determined to give the customer what they wanted, when I could, I poured the energy drink into a wine glass. There she was, judging her grandmother's potential for diseases, but she was making a social faux pas of pouring something other than wine in a wine glass. These kinds of things are so awkward for me to watch. It's cringy. Maybe it's proof of the different generations, or maybe showed how people are so out of social practice. However, no amount of social lubricant, which alcohol has shown itself to be, will be a cure for lack of class, or the lack of socializing.

It was being reported that the younger generation is drinking less in general now than ever. My philosophy is that with marijuana being more legal now, and it being easy enough to grow it yourself in order to get high without even having to socialize with a dealer or dispensary, this cheap alternative, is trumping the $60 bottles of wine and are making wine drinking much less appealing. It does, however, make me wonder if the granddaughter would have taken a drag off her grandmother's reefer in a multigenerational puff puff pass, or if all contact sports were off limits.

LIFE OR DEATH

J osh and Henry were working one morning when an old
model Cadillac parked in the driveway of Stonefruit
Canyon. The people in the car didn't come out right after
parking, but this was not unusual. Giving them some time to get
off the phone or send a text message, Henry and Josh kept
polishing glasses and getting the bar all stocked for the day.
Leaving the rest of the opening procedures to Josh, Henry
noticed the car was still parked, and he approached the Cadillac.

He offered to take a picture of the people in The Big Chair,
as that was often the reason people linger in front of the tasting
room building. They said that they were okay and didn't need a
photograph taken, but asked if they could use his phone to call a
family member. He handed the driver his cell phone, and the
woman took it, polished the screen clean with the edge of her
sweatshirt, gave Henry eye contact again, and then looked down
and dialed. During this time, Henry got a closer look at the two
other passenger. One man was older than him, and the other
woman was in her late twenties or early thirties. They all sat in
the car like they'd been there a while. Like their bottoms had
made a dent in the seat, similar to the settled in feeling one gets
during a long road trip.

Henry took two steps back to give the group some privacy
during the call, but it was his phone after all, so he stayed near
and did his classic arm lifting hand raise. The kind of wave
where his palm barely raises off his hip area, and definitely

doesn't bend much at the elbow. The friendly, but I'm not putting even more energy into this, as I'm already extending my comfort zone with you, kind of wave. The driver is mostly listening, but Henry does hear her say things like, "We're coming back from there," and "I don't know where that is" and when the two of them make eye contact again, the woman says, "I gotta go" and hands the phone back. Henry says, "If you need anything else, come see me inside," and points to the tasting room's front entrance.

Time goes by. Tasting room time is the kind of time where it's slower if you're slow, aka not many customers there, and faster when it's busy as you're tending to customers. It was a slower day midweek and therefore Henry went back to wiping down the bar, adjusting the blinds in the window, and giving Georgia some gentle pets.

However, this quiet countryside was about to change drastically when he noticed the woman driver standing outside the vehicle with the old man. They were waiving at Henry from outside their car to inside the tasting room. He had been at the window at just the right moment, so he rushed outside. Well as fast as one can in well-worn New Balance 608's.

When he got out to the people, the man was visibly distressed and slumped down in the woman's hug-like embrace. Henry went to catch the man from falling, and when he did the man's body weight was much heavier feeling than his 160-pound looking frame. The man slumped more and more, then proceeded to empty his bowels out his shorts and all over Henry's shoes. He had died. A seasoned man, Henry has seen a few things in his time, but nothing quite like this. This was new. This was definitely not a common occurrence to a writing professor turned wine educator, and he knew that a mound of paperwork was to come, and how would he tell his wife what happened when she routinely asked, "How was work today,

Henry?" And most of all, how would he get over the fact that he should have known to direct them to an emergency room, if only he had known. If only he could be like TV doctor, Dr. House, and saw sickness in the man's face, if only he did something. Filled with many more, "if only's" Henry was given the afternoon off, and was left to think about all the alternatives.

CHOICE WINE

During a flight tasting, Henry had a customer who asked, "What's the difference between the products grown at the winery's estate, like why would you sell it and not use it?" Henry chuckled, and said, "Well, we sell the stuff we don't want in our own wine!" You see, it's this kind of discerning attitude is how wineries have the choicest wines in their bottles and cellar.

Devin became the TMI (too much information) server one afternoon. He has a customer who had made a Facebook group for Paso wine fans, who called out and asked Devin, "Hey man, what do you know about the history of the grapes here?"

Devin, having just taken a course at Cal Poly about Viticulture and one about Enology, happily stopped polishing a glass and matched the drinker's cadence and said, "Well man, I know a lot. I mean, I just learned a lot in this class I took at Cal Poly. It's a fairly new thing, well, relatively speaking, it's not like Old World wine at all. I mean, man, the story is partly due to Paso Robles not always being a grape growing region. Wine grapes were introduced to Paso by the Spanish conquistadors and Franciscan missionaries. They kinda used it to take over. I think it was Francisco Cortez who first cultivated the land. He was a priest, who they called the Spanish word 'padres,' up at the Mission in San Miguel."

His customer clearly only cared about one part of all that monologue and asked, "Padres? Cool, like the baseball team, right?" Devin, looked down at his worn in brown loafers which he wore sockless, smiled a tad, and returned his gaze to his customers with an air of contempt, putting up with their ability to drag his intellectual conversation to something about something he found so simpleton- sports. But ever-hopeful for a good tip, he found some enthusiasm in his voice and said, "Yeah exactly! Because the missionaries started in San Diego, like the Padres team."

Devin continued on, "Hey man, if you want to know more, their old fermentation vats and grapevine artwork can still be seen at the mission, just north of here. As their obviously popular wines got a reputation which began to grow, they moved to more official bottling their wine and selling it. Basically, becoming commercial winemakers. But this wasn't until the late 1880's. Before then, the wine region wasn't really known outside of church communities until the late 1960s and early 1970s, when a new generation of grape growers really did their own thing here." That was the thing about Devin, he has contempt for most of his customers, but he didn't answer with short "yes" or "no" answers as if he was bored or annoyed by them. He instead would always answer their question with a long-winded full answer showing off his knowledge no matter how perturbed he was by people's questions. He was skilled enough not to let his annoyance show, but we knew.

TMI SERVER MEETS TMI WINE GUY

B etty welcomed a customer into Stonefruit Canyon, with a nice, "Good afternoon, welcome in. What can I get cha' today" and the customer, who introduced himself as Jim asked for "an old vine zinfandel with oak aging." Betty replied "We have vines over 100-years old and cask many in French Oak barrels." Then Jim said, "Humm, and what about your sustainable farming practices?"

After Betty replied, "Well we grow the vines year after year, and some for those hundreds of years, we have proven ourselves to be sustainable. I don't see that stopping anytime soon." Jim told a story about Lineage Vinyards down the road, and how they do this and that with their zinfandels. Getting a sense that Jim can never have enough details about the wine and that Too Much Information is welcomed, he fit the description of a TMI wine enjoyer.

Thankfully Devin was there because when tasting room and production worker, Devin, encountered a TMI wine enjoyer, it was a match made in heaven, as Devin was a story teller. He could go on and on about the wine, characterizing it from others and even what he was wearing when he worked "crush" in the winery production facility during Harvest time. The thing is, is that Devin doesn't give the taster any time to ask more questions as he went on and on answering the first. This is a dream come true for TMI Wine Enjoyer Jim. As a newbie working in the tasting room, I enjoyed this much information from coworkers Devin and Henry who would do the similar type of talk.

At the other end of the bar, Devin made his way into the conversation with Betty. After a moment, TMI Jim asked Devin, "How do you know so much about wine?"

"I'm going to Cal Poly and majoring in Viticulture with an emphasis on production. I'm in my third year, and before that I studied enology at John Hancock in Santa Maria. Ya know, to get some cheaper college credits and all that. I wanted to get my feet wet and in the door with some work before I was 21, and the wineries let me work in their production facility early. I was eager to work and felt strong, and I guess that worked for me. I mean I did work hard. I was able to do all the things the older people did, but definitely did some more grunt work. Ya know 'cuz I was a kid. But I'm here now so it was worth it. I mean I earned come hands-on credit too, but also learned a lot about making wine. It's hard work and not so easy to explain the in the amount of time I have with you here, but it's fun to know so much and be around the culture of wine. I learned some tricks, or trade secrets, if you will. Some stuff is too hard to explain now, but yeah, tannins, tanks and filters, and fermentation, botrytis, brix, aeration, I've done it all!" he replied with the ever too subtle air of superiority. Betty's customer leaned towards Devin, and asked, "Tell me more?" At this, Betty pushed over the bottle of wine to Devin, signaling that he could take over the tasting experience as they clearly had a connection, and Betty had had enough of Devin's mansplaining.

UNDER 21

O nce, a cute moment came from Liberty, daughter of Betty's friend Nina. Liberty, being a toddler in her mom's arms could easily be rested on the wooden bar while her mom chit chatted with Betty. Trying to involve Liberty with the hang out sesh, Betty asked, "Hey Liberty, smell what's in this glass and tell me what it smells like okay?"

Liberty shyly turned away and then was coaxed by her mom to participate with her Auntie Betty's question. She coyly turned to the glass and put her nose near the opening, "Mama it just smells like grapes like in my lunchbox at preschool!" The two women laugh, and they said, in unison, "That's right!" However, this is less cute when grown up customers sample the wine and say, "It tastes like grape juice!" Unless they are indeed trying to be funny, because it makes us think that we need to ask to see their ID again.

PUT A SPELL ON YOU

Sharon worked at Stonefruit Cellars' behind the scenes, in the offices at the production facility. She had witchy vibes, and was married to a drummer whose band name you instantly forget the moment they told you. The band name let me think he and his band members must smoke a lot of pot and wear a lot of black, but that's all I remembered about it. Sharon was an empath picking up on people's douchiness. Outside of work she was a girl scout leader, runner, mother to one. She gave off an anxious aura, and was likely on psychiatric medication. Her pet peeves were when customers hold the wine glass by the goblet cup part of the glass, which some called 'the bowl.' She knew the stem was there for a reason — our hands go around it elegantly and don't warm up the glass of chilled white wine. She was also peeved when customers touched the rim of the glass or have thick lip gloss that leaves goopy impressions on the glass. The gloss could be flavored and effect the tasting experience, and it was a pain to wash off. Even our high end dishwaser didn't wash it all off clean.

Sharon is the type of hard worker who dreams of wine, but had nightmares about wine. She confided in me that she had a nightmare one night as she was worried about work so much it was making her sick. I asked what her nightmare entailed, and she said, "It's silly. It would never happen." I gave her the look that I hoped said, "Come on friend, tell me." To which she replied, "Alright Jenn...I dreamed we were working on a weekend and we ran out of glasses!" I smiled and said, "Well we certainly wouldn't run out of wine!" and she shook her head slightly and said, "Well yeah, but the dishwasher takes 45 minutes and we totally ran out of glasses to serve people. It freaked me out. You know what? I am going to tell Betty we need to order more."

Sharon cared a lot. Working with kids always made her emotional. The kids would be with their inattentive-due-to-too-much-wine-parents and would get themselves in situations where only Sharon would be attentive and fix the situation. There were kids jumping on rattan furniture and tipping the balance of the chair in such a way that they fell off of the chair. There were kids who went upstairs and didn't know how to hold on to the stair railing handle when coming down and tripped and fell. These would all make Sharon emotional and upset as it reminded her of her daughter. Another pet peeve she has was when people make sounds while drinking, or even worse chew loudly at the bar. She also hates when people's tongue stuck out in weird ways. She made this abundantly clear one afternoon she was at the bar and had a customer who was a loud chewer and loud sipper. He was too much for her. He also needed to be taught that when tasting you either like the wine, or don't, and if you don't you can discreetly dump it in the dump bucket. If with a close friend you can offer it to them, if you wish. The most important thing to bring with you to Paso isn't your fanciest handbag or tales of exotic vacations, it's having an open mind about the wine. This can lead you to being surprised by something you thought you were closed off too. A lot of thought went into the tasting, so it's only fair to give it a try, but please, think of Sharon and others with misophonia, the aversion to eating sounds, and do it discretely. Give yourself the opportunity to connect with the passion behind the bottle.

Her tender side stood out even more as her exterior hinted at the fact she was likely goth in high school. She dressed like a Gemini. Her Doc Martin boots paired with lacy babydoll dress were so 90's that they must have come from her original high school closet, and not the teenage trendy section of Target. Her long straight gleaming blonde hair was more Barbie dream girl than Goth, but with some imagination and hair gel, she likely rocked out in the mosh pit of X-Fest or The Vans Warped Tour. I once heard her customer tell her, "I'm not drinking. I'm tasting," and her quick reply, "A rosé by any other name would smell as sweet" nodding to her Shakespearean knowledge and way she romanticized her life, with a little bit of edge.

A CASE FOR CASES

On days when Adrian does stay for hours, he certainly gets attention. He connects with all of us, Betty, Josh, Ambrose — and yes, me. He taps into that personal connection where the magic happens. It's complex genuine connection but not deep yet. We know it's near surface level, but there's an unwritten understanding about places like this. Places where people come for a good time. Places where people are not working, and not at home. It's the Third-Place notion where people get to be themselves and be liked for it. For many this feeling is foreign as they only stick to their workplace where people don't know them and don't like them, or home where they are known and not liked as one deserved. These Third Places tap into this kind of instant friendship magic which erases all discomfort and goes past small talk to create connection.

Most of the time, this friendship magic helps the hours go by faster and faster. But for some, these hours are business opportunities. The tasting room manager at the moment, Tammy, was an opportunist. What Tammy notices first is that customers linger, drinking ever so slowly. She seems welcoming to those who do this, but also sees someone who can help the winery's bottom line numbers. She has no reservation approaching him with the weekly specials on cases of wine. She doesn't think a single man needs to bring home 12 bottles of wine, but it is pure commerce, and not actually based on his needs, but hers. She sees an opportunity to make a sale, and, Adrian, not wanting to disappoint, went for her sales pitches. I have never worked with such strong women before and I was learning a lot from Tammy and Betty in this role. I also reflected on how the cats, Georgia and Sophia were teaching me subtle lessons too. I noticed how they just had to be cute and they were loved on and cared for. I was functioning more like a dog. I would sit pretty and do tricks like shaking hands and rolling over to get attention and earn a treat. These cats didn't have to do that to receive affection. They were not people pleasers and viewed themselves as the ones who needed pleasing. I would open the door to the tasting room for them over and over again. I would fluff up their beds in the cellar. I wondered if this is where the term "work like a dog" originated. That kind of work felt unsustainable, and I wanted to be more cat-like.

Sometimes after giving the cats tuck tuck at the end of the night, there might be some bottles of wine that needed tending to. These would be bottles that maybe are going home with a lucky employee, or maybe they are bottles that needed to be "married" as during the busy day we had opened two of the same white wine bottles that could now become one bottle for a worker to take home. Marrying the bottles means looking at the labels and checking they're the same exact wine and vintage year. Then examining the bottle contents, and picking the bottle with the least amount in it, and pouring it in the bottle with the most in it. There you have it — you married the bottles. Now, one might expect that we have funnels on the kitchen for this, but we don't. I had looked and looked again. I asked Henry, "Hey Gramps, why don't we have funnels for this task?" He smiled with the kind of confidence from living on this earth for nearly 70 years can provide, and replied, "We don't need funnels, because we're *professionals.*" I did feel like a liquid pouring professional now more so than ever. My pouring skills did improve and I was marrying the bottles like a Pastor on a Saturday during wedding season.

SPIT

I begin nearly every wine tasting experience off by welcoming customers in, and asking the customers, "Where are you visiting from?" as the majority of the customers are tourists traveling from out of the area, and asking them about their travels is a good conversation starter, and connection-maker. We've had people from all of the world visit us, although the majority were from Southern or Northern California.

One day as usual, the customers reviewed the menu and ordered a tasting flight as I placed the glasses out in front of her and the others in her group. I reached for the chilled Chardonnay from the mini fridge behind the bar, and poured it. A female customer looked disgustedly at the glass, and said, "I normally don't like Chardonnay," then stared at me blank faced. I suggested that maybe ours is different from others they have tasted. Plus, if she doesn't like it, I would not be offended. I pointed to the silver spittoon buckets and said she could pour the rest into one of those, and I'd get her the next offering from the tasting flight menu.

I felt this was a moment of confidence from me. I didn't get all hung up on pleasing her taste buds. I served her what she asked for, and I relinquished control over her enjoyment of the situation. I didn't personalize it. In the past when I had been told the details about people's headaches, that they "get from the sulfites in the red wine" I asked how they cared for themselves and what made them feel better. I lead with too much empathy when I took their suggestion that we carry over the counter headache medication. I like relinquishing control of people's entire experiences in our presence, and loved this newly confident side of me. Repairing and rebuilding self-esteem made me more confident in taking care of myself and others. It manifested as no longer chasing validation.

SIP BY SIP

Please, keep your reactions similar to how one behaves at an art gallery. This can mean the best behavior is to notice that someone made that and try to understand what they were doing, or working with what they were given. As wine is natural and begins with a plant that grew, it's fair to think about it in a similar way as it was crafted from materials and the maker added knowledge and experience to the piece. If your wine smells like citrus fruits, be specific and say lemon or marmalade instead of simply "citrus." If the wine smells like something from the earth, called "earthy" you can be ultra specific and say, "potting soil" or "wet gravel" to really impress.

Exaggerated expressions like shaking your head, are best a bit subdued. The person working in the tasting room likely didn't have a part of making the wine, so they're not offended if you don't like it, but try to be gentle and tactful. The worst thing you can do is spray the wine out of your mouth in disgust. Flat out calling a wine disgusting or sticking your tongue out are not classy behaviors. The tasting room is the gallery, the wine is the art. You are free to dislike it. This is more than just being classy. It's about respecting the hard work that goes into each bottle. If you truly do suspect there's something wrong with the wine, and that it's not just a matter of preference, it's okay to say something. You can ask your server if they "don't mind double checking this bottle, please" and follow up with a softly-spoken question about the possibility of it maybe being corked.

Corked is a term for when the wine's cork has

trichloroanisole, called TCA for short, in it. It's an off-putting type of contamination that affects the wine's aroma. You can tell this right away when the wine has a musty cardboard, wet newspaper, or wet dog aroma to it. I list all those as the smell is different to everyone, but once you learn what it is, trust me, you'll never forget it. It's impossible for this to happen to bottles capped with an aluminum cap as TCA is only present in actual cork. In the tasting room we are trained to check wines for this when we open the bottle. When opening a new bottle, you'll see your server open the bottle and pour a little bit of the wine into their own glass, and smell for TCA., and then pour the wine from the glass into the dump bucket if it's good and if it's been tainted by TCA. This method is the most accurate way to smell to check if the bottle is "corked" as simply smelling the cork is not accurate enough. We were trained that about one out of every two cases of wine, which is 1 in 24, have been corked, so we definitely know to check for it, but we can miss it sometimes if our sinuses are clogged or if we ate something pungent-smelling or tasting right before our shift.

Even if the wine is perfectly healthy, in the tasting room we understand not all wines will be liked by all people in all situations. If you don't like a wine, simply dump it out into the spit bucket. Feel free to express your opinion with respect to the environment. Wine is subjective, and we never blame a customer for having a certain preference. If you don't like a wine, be honest, but also be willing to try new flavors and styles. Being open minded means having an open palate. Communicating your preferences is important. It's also important to know know sometimes even the biggest wine lover has funky taste buds on different day. So, you're taste buds may simply not be in a wine tasting mood that day. This happens, so just notice the difference and refrain from judging yourself, or the artist, too harshly.

Also, don't be afraid to take small little sips, or medium size sips that you spit out in the spit bucket receptacle. A wine tasting series, called flights, generally have 4-5 tastes, but may include up to seven wines. To really evaluate the complexities of them, you don't need to fully drink them all to know if you like them or not. This is especially true if you plan multiple stops to different tasting rooms on that same day. It's very easy to over-whelm your palate which makes everything end up tasting the same.

Most wineries, like Stonefruit Cellars, are what is called a Counter Service establishment. This means that there's a different way to get service than at sit-down restaurants. At counter service places, you check in, are welcomed, order, are served, and pay at the bar. Now, if you do want to enjoy your picnic outside that's totally okay and welcomed, but still do it in the right order — counter ordering, paying, and then seat yourself.

Meaning after you order a bottle of wine at the bar, you then sit at the tables. If you went directly to the backyard's table and sat down, it may be a while before you're served as we didn't know you were out there, or if we did see you, we may assume you're our coworker's customers and may not notice for too long that you need customer service.

ATTRACTION GRATIFICATION

Delayed gratification is a skill psychologists revere. It's even called *The Art* of Delayed Gratification, which implies that there's many ways to do it and it can be beautiful. Eating crab is a prime example of delayed gratification. One must use tools, tiny forks and tiny crackers used to dissect and take apart the crab legs and body. It's an act of patience and gentleness. Taking the soft succulent meat out of the body and onto the fork for enjoyment is part of the process. It's the only joy you get during the process. There are many ways to eat the deliciousness after this. One can make a pile of the meat and savor it all at once after adding it all together in a juicy buttery pile on your plate. Developing the patience to work for something, and enjoy it all at the end is part of resisting immediate pleasure. Immediate bites would give you a sample of the deliciousness and it's often hard to work smoothly and slowly after taking that first same bite. But, the slow process of waiting to savor the delectable morsels is an investment. Investing in one's future happiness this way, is an act of discipline with one's focus on the goal. The goal of a delicious meal and happy dance on one's tongue. Don't get me wrong, the act of devouring the crab meat is enjoyed either way, but the slow and savory method is an act of delayed gratification that shows patience and makes the long-awaited bites worth it in the end. How is this connected to wine, you may ask? Well, wine isn't ready to drink right after it's made and for many, this is part of the enjoyment too. It's about the wait for the oak or other vessel to do its job and make that juice into wine. I love worth the wait moments.

For me, on the evening of the 46 West party there was a moment like that that tested my patience for delayed gratification. Having just worked together at the event representing Stonefruit Canyon and pouring wine for patrons, I was riding in Josh's truck, Big Red, and we were alone. Our bodies had worked hard lifting, loading, and unloading the materials for the event and we were done working for the evening. We let out a proverbial sigh of relief, a bit of satisfaction for finishing that day's work. The bonding over the shared experience could have been it. The moment to take a liiiiiitle nibble. I noticed it all. My senses were working overtime. On this ride, on the vineyard roads in a romantic pick-up truck could have been the moment to scooch closer to the driver's seat and kiss Josh. To take that little bit of what I was hungry for. I yearned to act on my impulses and get close to Josh. His close talking meant that he had already leaned in and I had been inches from his coy smile and beautiful pink lips before, but this time, I could reciprocally lean in and blame the bumpy road if the kiss wasn't welcome. I had daydreamed the kiss a hundred times and imagined it would have been a moment out of a country song riding in the backroad in a red pickup truck.

But, and there was a big but, I couldn't take that risk. I couldn't let myself enjoy that. I had a partner at home. We were going to couples therapy, and working on things. Plus, it would be risking my job and my work friendships. Plus, what if I enjoyed it? What if I really enjoyed it. Could I then handle the emotions that kiss could bring up to the surface? The other risk, and it was a big one, what if Josh didn't kiss back. Plus, the bump-in-the-road excuse could only work so well if it was actually a bumpy road, but Anderson Road wasn't as hilly as it would need to be to pull this off.

I marinated in this temptation to take in his young-millennial charm, and inhale his wine breath and touch his lips with mine. I wanted to know so much about wine and people but he in particular was so fascinating to me. His petite syrah-stained lips could be the cherry on top of this experience of coming into myself again. The real immersion into this industry. Josh represented a liaison, a guide in this re-coming-of-age story I was living. He was someone who taught me things. He taught me how to be a tad more subtle with my excitement about opening a bottle of wine just right, and how to properly hold a wine glass when smelling the wine's aroma. Most importantly he respected me and made my hours of work go by in a breeze. How could I not kiss someone who did that to me? I thought of my affinity for the crab metaphor and the benefits to delayed gratification and was tempted to bite into the deliciousness. Acting on impulse can come easy like easting fast food but leave you hungry after you come down from the sugar high. I wanted the bite, I craved the taste of it, but what I really needed was the whole meal. I knew he couldn't do that for me. He would be the one Pringle, when I wanted the whole tube of salted chips. This process of getting to my fill was slow and dainty.

At this point, my good judgement of the complex consequences saved me from making a mistake and taking a bite…or kiss. I also lacked the trust in my gut and struggled with picking up on signs. Of course, I had used my intuition before and these days I felt different. I was a new woman. A woman with a job where people said "Thank you" and a job where immediate gratification made dopamine hits when someone tipped me for my Forbes-approved customer service. I remembered my partner at home, and looked at the signs from Josh again with a clear head the next morning. Him having us pose for a photo together could have just been, "I'm a good boss" vibes, but they also could have been similar to the flirty nature I saw my co-worker engage in many times at the bar. It was a hard time being in my head and heart this season. I would lay awake at night and wonder would this part-time job lead me to a little fun fling? The guilt for even thinking about Josh in this way sunk in. I was scrolling Instagram and came across this quote from playwright Tennessee Williams who spoke of love and life when he said, *"The fact that we continue to fall in love with people or ideas and places is not evidence of our cupidity or our dumbness, but our strength. When we love...really love...in any way, we are announcing to the world that we intend to survive."*

That hit hard. You see, I truly was determined to survive. I wanted to survive and thrive. I was dedicated to self-discovery. I want to be blossoming like a flower, and be more self-aware during my second coming of age. I loved being in the tasting room working and serving others while also learning so much about wine and people, every day. I loved living where people vacationed. I loved discovering new interests and connecting to my past when a customer said they were from LA or the Bay. I loved myself and what it means to be myself as a partner and mother, but also as a whole capable human who was screaming to the universe that she wanted to live. Despite the electromagnetic strength of attraction, I put my longings aside. I was too practical-minded for a fling and I was nearly 10 years his senior. Plus, I knew crab tasted better when it was served with a big side of delayed gratification. Fret not, for when it was my turn to eat, and love, there would be no crumbs left.

PIT STOP

We had a family that would visit us monthly. Penelope and Zach lived in the Central Valley and would make trips to the beach and do a pit stop at their favorite wineries along the way to the coast. They would taste what's new on our menu and buy a couple bottles to enjoy later. It was common to have customers join our wine club, then stay in the club a year or so, then become members elsewhere. But from their member history that's saved in our computers, it showed they were consistent members for years. Their favorite wines were our cabernet sauvignon, malbec and port.

I was glad to have met, and poured wine for them. They had a son about my son's age and a baby daughter. Their cute family is probably what made me happy to pour for them as I daydreamed about being a family like that. A family that took leisurely vacations together and could travel with friends. They would share their love of our wine with their friends and booked a reservation for their friend's birthday at the winery. The following month it was Penelope's birthday and they made a reservation and specifically wanted me to pour for them. I was so flattered. Since I had built a rapport with them in these few months, I felt like I should do something special for Penelope, so I came up with the idea that I could make her a flower crown headband to wear. I handmade this crown with fresh flowers growing around the tasting room affixed to the headband with floral wire from the craft store. When Penelope and family arrived for their reservation, I presented her with the crown and she put it on right away. She was so expressively happy that I had treated her to a thoughtful gift. I thought Pablo from the Forbes training would be proud of my creativity in crafting a custom experience for our guests, and I was happy to have made her day.

FAVORITE CUSTOMER

Something shifted since the Cheers television show where "everybody knows your name" was a great sign of you mattering enough to remember between shifts. Let me explain, it became apparent not everyone wants to be noticed as a regular, or person who frequently comes to the winery.

When out and about in downtown Atascadero, I recognized a customer I had poured for many times. So many times, in fact, I felt comfortable making eye contact with the woman and saying "hello." The woman replied with a shy "hi" and I said, "I work at Stonefruit Canyon and remember you from the tasting room there."

The woman said, "yeah I guess I may have been there before." Returning back to her brew at Ancient Owl, I felt something was different with this interaction and chalked it up to social awkwardness that introverted people had. I couldn't shake the feeling of confusion and wondered if one of the friendliest and least socially awkward guys who I knew also had the same thing happen. When I went to my next shift at Stonefruit Canyon, I asked Josh if that ever happened to him before. He sighed, and said that the same sorta thing happened inside the tasting room itself. One day Josh saw a customer coming in the tasting room, and said, "Oh look, it's our favorite customer, you!" the customer was visibly uncomfortable and said, "Huh? Me?" Josh went on saying, "I recognize you from Side Street Bar and Grill on the square…or was it Silva Brewing? Anyways, we're both in the Mug Club!"

The same awkwardness came over the man Josh recognized. Clearly, there's some social-drinking unwritten rule, inside or outside the tasting room. What Josh said was right, for as tasting room workers, we did have favorite customers. The ones who know the bar can be a fun place to hang out, but that it's a sacred space that doesn't transcend place. Perhaps then, tasting rooms are taking on a bit of that Vegas motto "What happens in Vegas, in fact, stays in Vegas."

To get recognition and move to the top of our very unofficial Favorite Customer List, lead with respect and if we go out of our way and call a restaurant to get you a table, or other winery, to get you an exclusive reservation, say "thank you" by tipping, or let your words speak for themselves and leave a Yelp or Google review. There's a lot of power in this position of wine educator. Because we're working here sober it's likely that we will remember you and if you were rude, we may even go out of our way again to recognize you in public one day. And if you were super rude, we may even purposefully call your partner by the wrong name just to instigate a fight between you two.

On the other hand, I can take note of something special going on in the vineyard that I can include on the tour; to give a truly unique hands-on tasting room experience.

I learned we can do all this, all the right things and things still can go wrong. But it doesn't always matter if it's wrong. This felt like life outside the tasting room too.

No matter how it's going at work, I could always have the possibility of having my favorite customer show up and turn my day around. I can always rest easy knowing that when I messed up telling a small detail about the wine that the customer was probably a wee tipsy, and won't exactly quote me on that. There was power in working in an environment like this too. I could seat people who are acting like my least favorite customer to be quick at their tasting, if I sat them outside on a day that's too dang hot and I was feeling a tad spiteful on the inside.

RAISE YOUR SPIRITS

One evening after work some coworkers and I wanted to check out the nearby distillery. I made sure others were joining me and Josh this time, so it wasn't awkward like long ago. These kinds of distilleries have been popping up all over recently in efforts to attract something else for 21+ and older customers to imbibe in while in Paso.

We all drove our separate cars as we didn't want to have to carpool and time our departures together. We planned this as they were open an hour later than us, so we all conspired to do the closing procedures really quickly, in order to get over to the distillery fast after our closing time, giving us the most time at the distillery. So, in the parking lot at our nearby destination, we reconvened and could admire our workplace from a new angle as the distillery was uphill from the rolling vineyard. We entered and there was a hipster type working there. You know the type, beanie, skinny jeans, and pride from riding his bicycle uphill (both ways!) to work. I wondered how much he'd judge us from all driving our cars one quarter of a mile from work to here. We all posted up to the bar, and Betty lead the conversation saying that we all work at Stonefruit Canyon. Henry chimed in and said, "Oh, I thought we were going to tell him we were a Mötley Crüe of a family? Shucks." I could tell this was going to be a fun hour for us right away. The server asked if we wanted the tasting menu, or knew what kind of cocktail we wanted. Experienced Josh spoke up and told them that none of us had been here before, so we should all try a tasting flight. We were all given glasses, the short and stout kind, with bulbous bottoms that feel good in your hand and are often used in whisky tastings.

As we sipped, we learned that they use the byproduct from the wine making process to make grappa, something that they specialize in. "That's great recycling!" I exclaimed in a way that later made me blush as I felt I was revealing my sustainable nature. There was a different grappa to try, one that was casked, meaning held in an oak barrel that had previously been used for whisky. This barrel made the grappa a bit more smokey, heavy, and fruity all at once. It was delicious and helped us warm up to the next one that was truly divine. The flight ended with a drink called Nocino. We learned it was made from walnuts on the family's property. Another resourceful move, I thought, but I kept this to myself, understanding not everyone is motivated by thoughtful stewarding.

Nocino tasted like Christmas in a bottle. It was room temperature, but felt like a warm hug from Santa. I love a beverage like this during wintertime, and felt it would be perfect paired with a cozy blanket and fireplace. I told the server I wanted to buy a bottle, and my frugal nature came out again, when I asked for the industry discount, which is often 10-40% off retail prices. That's worth asking about, if you ask me. I was told their discount for those in the industry is 25% and I found that satisfying. As I concluded my transaction, I heard Josh and Betty's conversation of where to go next. Henry stepped out of this plan right away, when he said, "Go have fun you guys. I'm out." I was questioning if I had another stop in me, but I knew my son was waiting at home for me and I would like to do his bedtime routine with him. I also really needed to keep saving my money so I can afford my own apartment. So, I regretfully told the group that I had my drink for later, while holding up the bottle, and would not be hanging out later tonight. I said my goodbyes and headed towards the exit. I hear Betty invite the bartender, officially named the spirits educator, and I guess they all felt called to join up at a bar in downtown. I could only imagine the night they all got themselves into.

BUT IT'S MY BIRTHDAY

The next weekend I came to work and said hello to everyone by saying, "Good morning, Party People!" I got further in the tasting room, I saw it was just Ambrose working in the tasting room. He was polishing glasses, and from the kitchen window we saw a tourist van pull into the parking lot. There was also a Ford Expedition behind them. I noticed, "There must be a big reservation this morning!" Ambrose told me, "Yeah, I think it's a birthday celebration," and just then we saw a gaggle of girls get out of the Ford Expedition and the van. Hurrying to polish the glasses, we saw them approach the tasting room entrance but get a bit distracted along the way. First by Georgia, who was strutting through the parking lot. She beckoned all of them to pet her by her sheer poofiness and friendly nature. And then secondly, the girls were distracted by the big chair. They all seemed to know how this would work with their large purses and even bigger hats. How their shawls would hang and favorite angles would be just right for the camera as they put their best face forward. It was funny to see who chose to hold their purse for the photo and who would hide their purse on the ground by the chair. Being a purse gal myself, it seemed to be a choice of designer and size. Larger hobo type bags from Macy's made their way to the ground, and smaller designer logoed ones would get the right to sit next to them, or even stay on their shoulder or cross body position. After the group photo's obligatory "silly one" and "serious one" they all got off the chair and gathered themselves together. You see, it took a bit of athleticism to get up on the chair, and especially when wearing oversized and fashionable clothing.

We opened the front door to be more welcoming, and saw one girl who lingered on the chair. She told her friends she wanted a solo picture. A friend grabbed her phone from her, and another she offered to hold her bag for her. She went into a loud voice, and we could hear her yell, "Bitch, this bag IS my outfit. I'm not setting it down! Now, hurry up and take the picture, there's wine to drink!" Ambrose and I both chuckled, and as a girl with handbag day dreams, I understood.

The gaggle of girls made it into the tasting room, and we welcomed them by saying, "Hi, Welcome to Stonefruit Canyon" simultaneously. They walked to the bar, and knowing how important their bags are, I pointed out the purse hooks conveniently located on the front of the bar. They were so excited, smiling and ogling Ambrose's preppiness and one said, "I knew I liked it here!" I laid out the tasting menus in front of them, and Ambrose went into his usual spiel about the tasting menu options. One asked, "Is it true that my tasting is free if it's my birthday?" Ambrose smiled, and asked, "IS it your birthday?"

"Well, it can be...it almost is. Yes" she replied. Ambrose replied, "Well, what I can do is waive your tasting fee when you buy two bottles of wine..." and added "and I'll sign the bottle for you." The girls giggled, and I knew Ambrose had control of the bar and its gaggle of patrons, so I went back to the kitchen to tend to polishing the wine glasses and hopefully finding Georgia to pet. She was the most excellent therapy cat, and I could tell the bar was about to be raucously loud in no time.

RETURN CUSTOMER

A drian comes back time and time again to the tasting room. His presence transcends the usual customer, as he's become a regular. As a regular, he goes past the barrier from customer to friend. So, as a friend, one Saturday he brings all of us working Cranberry Bliss Bars from Starbucks. Getting everyone's Starbucks order is harder as people's drink tastes are so different, so instead he knows that everyone loves the seasonal delight that is the Cranberry Bliss Bar. If you've never had one, you need to know they are a chewy dessert bar, topped with cream cheese frosting and dried cranberry and orange zest. They combine sweetness from chocolate chips and tartness from the cranberry and frosting and are so delicious, as anything with butter usually is. Starbucks sells them individually as triangles, and also as a large rectangle in a sharing-size tray. Personally, I think they pair with nearly all wine better than they pair with coffee. If you're looking to pair them you have many options. Namely port which has a dessert sweetness to it, and merlot as they share fruitcake tendencies, and even chardonnay as they meet with the similar buttery and citrus notes. Basically, they're delicious as all hell, and it's a shame they're only available seasonally. In the tasting room, we all loved this delicious treat.

Adrian does a lot of other things right, not just generously treating us to a box of Bliss Bars. He finds ways to tip us that don't feel unfair as he couldn't possibly give a cash tip to everyone working, but since they all interact with him, they would be deserving of it. So, he found some ways to give us all a treat instead. Sometimes with snacks, and sometimes with being helpful with other customers. He talks to other customers which relieves us from having to entertain the bar every minute, and he's relatable and funny. He knew when a joke would be too much and he doesn't go there, ever. He doesn't joke if he can sip from the dump bucket, claiming that "alcohol kills germs" like others joke about. He doesn't wear cologne which alters the smell around him which can affect the tasting experience of those around him, as we know the nose is a large part of the tasting experience. He doesn't make faces when tasting the wine. He does however smile in a way that crinkles the corners of his eyes at me. Admittedly, he's a feast for the eyes as he gets better looking the more you look at him. I wondered what had gotten into me. There was something about him that made me believe him when he said he liked something. He said things like, "I like that zinfandel you poured for me," he personalized the compliment. I noticed him saying the "that you" part and started to wonder which he liked more, me or the wine.

He heard I was a fan of Starbuck's egg bites and made it his new hobby to learn how they're made. He said he had bought a sous vide machine and was trying different recipes but hadn't figured it out yet. Betty asked him one Saturday, if he was going to bring in these sous vide egg bites he was working on. Adrian said, "Not yet, they're not perfect enough for Jenn yet!" She started to get suspicious that he may have a crush on me. While working in the cellar, she asked, "Hey you know that Adrian customer? I think he has a crush on you! He's been learning to cook those egg bites you like and I'm sure even the imperfect ones are good, but he won't share them with us until they're truly perfect for you." She emphasized *you* and while this did feel like a good cover for my crush on Josh, both of these men were forbidden fruits to me. I couldn't even humor the thought of my heart opening to a man when I desperately was working on things with my son's dad, and preparing my bank account to leave if things wouldn't work out. It wouldn't be from our lack of trying, and my savings was growing in the meantime.

Despite my closed heart, I wasn't the only one picking up on Adrian's flirty admiration. I overheard a customer once ask him, "Is there something going on between you two," as she pointed to me. Adrian cooly replied, "Oh no, not yet. But one day we'll get married and honeymoon in Paris together!" The customer laughed off the audaciousness of his comment, and they continued sipping wine at the bar.

PICKUP PARTY

"Wine & friends are a great blend." -*Ernest Hemingway*

L eading up to the pickup party, Adrian was back at the tasting room's right side of the bar and he asked to buy extra tickets to the party. He explained that he wants to invite his two best friends to tag along with him. He's proud he's convinced his friends Emery and Aaron to finally hire a babysitter for their kiddos and get out of the house for the evening. The wine club member party is scheduled to be at the winery production facility, just north west of the tasting room. Adrian tells me he and his friends are coming and they'll carpool together and that she's a big fan of wine. Her husband, his best friend, is learning to like wine but for now is more of a beer and whisky guy. I tell him that he's welcome to bring guests, and I am curious about his friends as he makes friends so easily at the bar. He buys their tickets and offers to tip as he's seeing others around him do that sometimes. But as much as I am motivated by earning money, I feel there's something different in these interactions with him. It's hard to pinpoint exactly, but it's more of a friendly feeling than customer and wine educator feeling. I tell him it's okay, he doesn't have to tip us, and I am thankful he doesn't make it awkward by insisting.

On the day of the party, I came into work like I always walk into the tasting room by saying, "Goooood morning Party

People!" to my coworkers. This greeting started as a fun way to say hello that greeted the group of coworkers who I noticed brought the party wherever they went or were recovering from the last party they went to. It also helps to let my workers know it's me opening the tasting room doors and not an early customer, so they could remain seated in the back room.

On this day we all knew we were closing the tasting room early around 3PM and would all drive to the winery production facility to set up tables, tablecloths, and wine galore for the second half of our day — the wine club pickup party. This party would be catered and the owners would be there to give speeches and help give prizes to attendees. My job was to work a bar that was set up on the right side of the barrel room near the wine barrels and merchandise display booth. I bought new shoes for the occasion, knowing I'd wear them to work if they worked out at the party too. This was a tad out of character for me, as I value comfort so much. I also didn't need new shoes as my Nike's were working just fine, but something in me sparked when I saw these fringed leather boots in Boot Barn's store window. I saw the boots and thought someone who's confident and beautiful wears boots like that. I figured they wouldn't even have my size, size 10, but if they did, I'd have to try them on. Well, they fit really well and were actually on sale. I would have to use my tips from the last three days to afford them, and this would set be back three days from being ready for a place of my own, but the feeling those boots gave me felt worth it. I took off my Nike's and wore the fringed boots for the first time as we headed to the pickup party.

I felt like a badass as I had been working at the bar, all set up with a variety of wines: zinfandels, a cabernet, our Bordeaux blend of course, as well as our malbec and petite verdot single varietals. In an ice bucket, I have a bottle of our new sparking wine. I love to keep a very tidy bar with paper towels and a trash can at the ready. I keep my wine key on my bar and one menu for the customers to see what we're pouring today. The bottles are usually lined up, so the customers can see the bottles and not just the wine list, for those visual learners. I am always a teacher and thinking about variations in learning. The great thing about these parties is that we are not charging people for each drink, as the cost of the wine is covered in their entrance ticket. This is lovely as it takes money out of the equation of service. Plus, it simplifies the interaction. I get to be generous, and charming without asking for people's money. You see, I do not have to use the iPad for this interaction at all. This releases all stress and my prayers hoping to God that the internet is working at this rural environment. This way, I wouldn't have to manually type in their credit card number as we did in the tasting room. While inconveniences like this were seen as quaint and quirky happenings in rural environment, it was pretty antiquated and less streamlined for the customer. So, all in all, I was thrilled when customers didn't have to pay for each glass of wine and we could charge for a few items at once.

In this happy environment, I could also be entertained as there was a live band playing, and I could also be educated as the winemaker and cellar manager were at this event and would be telling attendees what's so special about this particular vintage. I overheard him saying this is a 2019 vintage, and the malbec's so juicy and special and to not forget to try the petit verdot 2019 vintage next to the 2018 to notice the difference in the terroir that year. These were all new wines being released that night, and the buzz in the atmosphere was so excitable and celebratory all at once. This is exactly what people sign up for our wine club to enjoy. I was excited to try the wines myself, but am pretty strict about drinking alcohol at work and knew I could try them at home as the owners were gifting all of us workers a 6-bottle pack of the wines we were releasing at the party. Standing at my bar at the ready, I noticed a few regulars. I love seeing their familiar and friendly faces. Adrian walks in to the cellar room too. I smile and knew just what to pour him as I want to see his happy reaction to trying the newly released sparking wine, Pet Nat, which is short for Pétillant Naturel, and is an old school way of fermenting wine. It was the winery's answer to a sparkling wine which customers were asking for. This is a wine made here in Paso, but its style is a nod to the Champagne France is famous for. I think of how I am going to describe this wine as effervescent versus truly bubbly, and as I am thinking of how to describe the nose (it's smell), I see one very familiar face. It's my friend Emery who I know from the Moms Club of Atascadero. She and I lock eyes, and she approaches my bar and says, "Hi Jenn, I didn't know you worked here!" I replied, "Yeah, it's kinda new, just since last March." She said, "That's neat" and then introduced her husband, Aaron, to me.

Adrian excitedly pops in and says, "Wait, you two know each other?" And I come out from behind my bar to stand closer to my friend, say "Yeah, we're in Moms Club together. Our kids, well my son, and her oldest son, are friends." Aaron says, "Adrian, THIS is the Jenn you told us about?" as he looks at Adrian. Adrian looks at me and says, "Well yeah, it's the only Jenn I talk about!" And we all kind of awkwardly smile at each other and I am intrigued that I was being talked about.

Emery says, "Guys, there's so many people named Jenn, I didn't put it together it was YOU Jenn!" I smiled and got back to work behind the bar. I grabbed her a glass and also poured her some Pet Nat, Describing the Pet Nat was something totally new for me, but I thought maybe Emery would like to give it a go. I asked if she'd like to try it, "But no pressure on liking it, as there are plenty more options here tonight."

After pouring her some, I turned to Adrian and said, "Adrian, would you like the Chardonnay, or go straight to red wine tonight?" and Aaron looked at Adrian and chuckled, "Adrian? Who calls you that? You'll always be AJ to me." Adrian explained to us all, "Well, they asked me what my name was when I started coming here a lot. You know, after that Ugly Christmas Party I went to with you guys' last year? That's when I signed up for the wine club. And, this Spring I have been coming here on Saturdays. So, I guess I kind of worked out that I'm Adrian here."

Emery being keenly observant, says, "Well that explains how she didn't know that we knew each other. When she's come over with her son for a playdate it's always earlier than you would come over. Since you're 'Uncle AJ' to my kids, them talking about you didn't trigger even the idea that you are in fact the same man as Uncle AJ. Plus, I know a million women named Jenn. It's wild this is the same one!"

My eyes widened as I asked them, "Wait a second, you're bothers?" as I looked at both Aaron and Adrian/AJ in further amazement. Adrian says, "Oh no, my brothers are across the states. The two of us we were in the United States Navy together. We were on submarines. While we were underway on assignments, we got close. So, it's like we're brothers. Now we still work together like we did when we were in the Navy," Aaron explained.

Boggled, totally boggled, so I did what many do under pressure, I smiled, and said, "So you two are American Heroes" and I walked to the other side of the bar. I noticed how my new boots sounded on the concrete floor of the tasting room. They sounded strong. But, getting back to business, I pour Aaron some Pet Nat, and Adrian already had an empty glass and was ready for his next wine. I poured him our wine which is lightest in body, but is also our most aromatic zinfandel called, Pony Springs. I encourage them to take their wine and walk around a bit. They can have some bruschetta and meatball appetizers, meet Bruce the winemaker, and mingle with other wine connoisseurs.

I wipe my bar down and check my watch for the time. It was early in the night. I make sure the next wine is open and ready to go with its cork replaced with these little foil pieces we use which help the wine pour out in an elegant manor, while also helping to reduce drips. I also did some deep yoga breaths to center myself. These rituals have become part of my in between customers procedures. They keep me feeling calm and prepared.

After learning that Adrian is in fact not just a jovial lush, but actually someone I have mutual friends with, my mind softened to the possibility of pouring for him yet again. I am glad he's not simply a lush. But so many possibilities cross my mind. He spoke about me to them and I was curious what he said. Maybe Emery would invite him to a playdate we had for our kiddos, or maybe Emery would visit the tasting room again. Now that I know she likes wine, when we got together with Mom's Club, we would have a whole lot more to talk about. Since I was learning so much about wine, I was sure I could teach her about the local wine here. Plus, now that I see Adrian as her kiddos "Uncle AJ" there's so much more depth and intrigue than simply Adrian the man at the end of my bar. He liked kids. He liked cats and kids. These were certifiable green flags.

Later in the evening, I learn that as the honorary uncle, he's close with Aaron and Emery's two sons and loves to spoil them with loud toys for their birthdays and Christmas. I smile knowing that they added the descriptor "loud" to describe the toys, as Adrian being the uncle thinks it's funny when the parents are annoyed with the sounds toys make until their batteries run out, which always seems to last forever the more annoying the toy's sounds are. Best friends sometimes tease each other and I could tell this was the kind of camaraderie they shared.

THE BOOTS

One morning we were all called into the tasting room for a last-minute meeting. It was a very rainy day in March. I looked outside and saw it was raining those big dollops of rain that tap the windows as the wind pressed the drops on the glass panes even harder. Betty told me the meeting was at 11AM in the tasting room. I laughed as I told her I saw this horror film scene before — the mid-size white girl in the compact car always dies in the rainstorm at the beginning of the movie, so I am not coming in. She chuckled and said, "I get it! But really girl?" I sighed back, and in a more serious voice said, that I couldn't get childcare this fast, and wouldn't be able to come. She lamented and said she understood, and would talk to me later.

When I got off the phone, my son's dad said it was a good thing that I didn't go to work today anyhow. I cocked my head to the side, questioning why he'd say that, and he added, "Well those new boots you've been wearing to work make you a poser. You're too much of a city girl to wear those. They make you look fake because you're not country like I am." This was disorienting. He was country in that he had a strong work ethic, and we made it a tradition to eat a corn dog at the Mid State Fair, but I remembered him telling me he was born in Salt Lake City and lived in the suburbs of Seattle and Denver before moving to the Central Coast.

The more I thought about what he said, the more I noticed that he was pretty right. He was more country than me. His friends had let us fish on their property before, and he owned multiple tents and coolers. I was more city than him in that I could parallel park. But I liked, like really really liked my new boots. I figured as a Gemini I could wear boots, too. Especially since they were technically booties and went to my ankle. They were tan suede, but they didn't have designs on the toe or any rhinestones. All the feelings were juxtaposed to how I felt powerful, and beautiful in the boots. How I had scored a really good deal on them, and they didn't even hurt my feet, despite long hours standing in them.

Thinking back, I had lived in cities and suburbs most of my life before coming to the Central Coast over a decade ago too. Here, I even did country things like when I worked for a woman-run company that made t-shirts with country song lyrics on them. I travelled for the company selling the shirts at country music festivals in the Midwest. It made me wonder what kind of country cred I would need to possess to have the permission to wear boots to my job in the country. Maybe the fact I thought country cred was a thing that could even be obtainable proved I was a city girl that listened to a lot of hip hop. Well, if anything, I was a recovering city girl. When I reflected on my time in the wine industry, I noticed how this journey had changed me. I had just turned down work. I had really fit in at that job, and people liked me there. I had met some great and inspiring people. Being around my coworkers changed me. They changed me for the better. I had stood up for myself when I said I didn't feel comfortable going in to work. I stood up for my safety in the storm. I put my apron on and began my chores for the day. Feeling a smidge rebellious, I also put my boots on, too.

I knew I wanted to not only live, but I wanted to thrive. I asked myself what that meant to me and what I truly wanted. I wanted love. I wanted a full legit Hallmark Channel family. I wanted marriage, and I wanted a committed partner. I wanted a closet full of the shoes I'd wear as I'd have different sides of me. I wanted my education and cleverness to get me what I wanted. I wanted a wedding ring which represented a symbol of something so rare and so special — everlasting love. I wanted to give myself a chance at finding authentic love. I would fall in love with more than the boots. I was feeling good about my decisions and remembered I had control over my own story.

I had fallen in love with my new self. It was there, in that moment I knew I was done being a single mom in a complicated relationship. I had evolved. I wore fun clothes like fringed boots. I made a radical career move and made my dream of being a customer service worker a reality. I was on my way to being a woman who loves, and is loved in return. My son's dad thought everything was great between us. We were going to couples therapy and I had gone quiet. I stopped nagging him to be treated well. He didn't notice I had given up and was switching gears. I had my fringed boots on, I was literally an inch taller, but it was more than that that changed my perspective. I had confidence. And it was with my new confidence and I knew I could start anew again.

TWO WEEKS TO FLATTEN THE CURVE

I t's true what they say about being different people when you start dating, and when you break up. Feeling different inside, my home felt strange. I felt like I was a visitor in it. I'd dealt with awkwardness before, so I fought on and didn't give it too much thought as I had so many mental tabs open already. In the afternoon, I received an email recapping the meeting I missed — which was that the tasting room needed to close for two weeks. It wasn't due to the Heck's, but the government. This was scary change. I didn't understand why the government wanted to close the 300 or so wineries here. In the email, it was explained to us wine educators that this would be a temporary closure and to make up for the tasting room being closed, more hours of work were offered for us to do in the production facility.

I replied to the email saying I could take that as an opportunity to learn more about the production side of the winery. When I showed up to work, I noticed I had been the only one who opted to continue to work there. So, there I was; alone in a huge, I mean huge warehouse. Well, I wasn't totally alone, the owner's dog would run through from time to time. I was alone with bottles and cases of wine and even a forklift. I was told this was safe from the Corona germ as I was so far from another person. The work pile was enough to keep me company for some time, as the number of bottles we had to package up skyrocketed as orders increased.

Customers needed alcohol delivered to their home as they couldn't come to the tasting room and buy it themselves. But by then, as restrictions changed rapidly over those few weeks, people didn't even want wine delivered to them as they feared there were germs on the bottle and in the packages, and from their mailman. Also, to me, it began to feel pretty hard to think of the world ending, yet it was important to get someone their wine delivered to their door step.

I had to balance my dutiful nature with the notion that work was more a more valuable use of time than my own health and safety. So, during this time of financial insecurity and unprecedented awkwardness, I knew I had to leave. I did what human resources told me I could try to do. I filed unemployment and hunkered down at home with my son, his dad, and my dog Luna. We were hopeful we could ride out the thing that made us chuckle as it was named after a beer —Corona. I knew deep down that a sickness named after a wine wouldn't do people dirty like that.

One morning I woke up to a notification on my phone. It was a message from a 559 number, California's Central Valley's area code number, and read "Hi! I think this is your number Jenn, I found your number online. It's Penelope, a customer of yours at Stonefruit Canyon. I heard the tasting rooms are closed and my family and I would like to send you a little money to help you get by these two weeks. What's your PayPal?"

With tears filling up in my eyes, I confirmed she was right, it was me. I felt she was an angel for thinking of me, and told her that. I shared my email address associated with my PayPal, and a moment later when my phone pinged with the Notification, my tears overflowed from my eyes and dripped down my cheeks. I felt I wasn't alone. These semi-strangers liked me. Liked me enough to hunt me down and give me money.

There were some serious highs and lows during this Covid time. My life felt like the stock market with its booms and busts, or a flower with its thorns and roses. Basically, through the hibernation, I had felt like I had gone through the winemaking process myself. Like the floral buds that bloomed, I had to be stung to be fertilized and turn into a grape. Then as a wine grape, I had been crushed, juiced, and had gone through a lot of development and effort to become something even better. Then in a barrel, I fermented. This is where my strength was realized. I had been strong, but my experiences made me stronger. As time passed, I got stronger and stronger in my barrel. Getting stronger, yet softer on the palate, my essence had changed from grape juice to wine. Then, when it was time, I was poured from the wine barrel and into the bottle.

In the bottle, the experience of being homebound, I was crushed because things couldn't work out between my son's father and I. I was a recovering city girl, but this wasn't enough for the country-boy he was. Like wine, my life had been upside down, pumped over and pressed down. I had bottled up a lot of emotions, and the action helped me come out of my comfort zone like a shaken-up bottle of sparkling wine. When it was my time to come out of the bottle, I felt elation when I finally had enough belief in myself at the same time of having enough money. Often times money never coincides with time and confidence, but this wasn't one of those times anymore. I also had enough tip money, being the highest earner at Stonefruit Canyon, combined with my Coronavirus Aid, Relief, and Economic Security Act's (CARES Act) whose Economic Impact Payments were like gold. All this meant that I finally had enough money to pay first and last months' rent and security deposits on a place that not only accepted dogs, but even had a little yard for Luna, for I was definitely taking my dog to live with my son and I. I had done it. I used my money, and newfound confidence to love myself. I believed in myself. Reinvention wasn't just a fun option for me, it was a decision to survive, a commitment to thrive. I had done this for the future me, and for my son. I was a new me. A me I was going to be proud of. I had found my way back to myself. I was done working from the need to people please. I was done fawning. I was thriving.

"I love how wine continues to evolve, how every time I open a bottle it's going to taste different than if I had opened it on any other day. Because a bottle of wine is actually alive —it's constantly evolving and gaining complexity. That is, until it peaks [...] and it tastes so fucking good." - Maya, *Sideways* (2004)

NO RULES

I did it. I had left my son's father and moved into my own place across town. I felt like the wine-making process again. I felt like a bit of a badass, like ripe juicy grapes full of potential, I knew the pressuring crush was coming. I would have some different pressures put on me as I was now a single mother navigating the world of co-parenting and mothering a five-year-old. Inevitably, there was some bottle shock as I entered this new reality of my life. Mixed with the world's new reality of masks and vaccinations in this new frontier of a society, I had a lot to manage. Luckily, it felt like everyone else was struggling in one way or another too, so the collective vibe of, "What on Earth is this new normal?" made this transition easier. Everyone else had changed. Those who used to go out to see live music shows now had taken on birding. Those who were avoiding carbs started making sourdough loaves. If they could pivot, I could definitely change my life, too. Like many of us, we had been bottled up and longed for fresh air. Like wine again, I needed some time to breathe and swirl in a glass. I much preferred getting out of a barrel from the cellar and into a warm patio.

I felt good about who I was, I made good choices for myself. I refused to quit. Something had shifted in me. The first step of feeling good about ourselves is remembering the inherent power and control that we have over ourselves. It took time and hard work. But it was something I was familiar with as I had dedicated myself to self-discovery and self-improvement.

WHO RUN THE WORLD? MOMS!

I wanted to take my mom wine tasting for Mother's Day. I saw on their social media that Celestial Cellars was having a special for the holiday and invited patrons to bring a picnic and spend the afternoon in the winery's backyard. They promised to make it special and have a live band and free mini bouquets for all the moms with reservations. This sounded like a great way to spend the day, so I made a call to make a reservation. A friendly voice answered the phone, and I recognized her voice immediately as Betty from last year at Stonefruit Canyon. "Betty Hauser? It's me Jenn Luck! From Stonefruit Canyon." I could hear the smile in her voice when she replied, "Christmas, how the heck are ya?" It was her! I thought to myself, "What a small world this Paso wine world is?!" and we talked for a moment about how she started working there recently and hasn't heard from any management or any of the tasting room crew at Stonefuit Canyon anymore and wondered how Covid treated them. She also sounded excited that I wanted to make a reservation and would be coming the upcoming Sunday with my family.

The Saturday before I prepared for the picnic by making a charcuterie board fit for a queen. I matched tiny pickles called ghurkins, different cheeses like brie and gouda, with green grapes and water crackers. I even put honeycomb and placed it near the rose shape I made with layered salami. Pinterest eat your heart out! We would be indulging in style. We brought seltzer waters to accompany the wine we planned to drink as I know that's my dad's favorite beverage, a nod to his German heritage. Plus, I expected he wouldn't drink much anyways, given the strict guidelines on his pharmaceutical bottles. My mom and I were dressed in floral dresses and my son wore a button up shirt. He picked out the shirt on his own, as he said, "Today is going to be fancy" and he wanted to impress me and his grandmother.

We arrived to the tasting room after parking by stacks and stacks of barrels. The pastel house was darling, and I imagined a house turned winery would have the best stories. We were welcomed by Betty, and we exchanged "nice to see you" and a hug. Betty sat us in a prime location, under a big navy-blue umbrella between the tasting room and under the springtime sunshine. As I sat there and talked with my family, we were arranging ourselves to be cozy and enjoy our picnic and wine together. I looked over the menu Betty gave us, and decided we should share a bottle of wine, as that would surely be more than enough for the four of us. I knew that given the salami on our charcuterie board, my mom traditionally prefers white wine, so it being her day, Mother's Day, I opted for a white wine. Betty helped me pick from a few wines offered, by saying that their white Rhone-style blend is the best. It has picpul blanc, grenache blanc, and viognier grapes. I trusted her palate and judgement, and we went with that bottle. She brought it to us, and as she was opening the bottle and pouring it for each of us, she asked me if I missed working in the tasting room and if I could be interested in coming back to work. This time I'd be working for her, as she was the tasting room manager. I was instantly flattered and asked what's it's like there with the Covid rules of mask wearing indoors and everything. She told me that "With the tastings being outside we don't have to wear masks when pouring, and that the owners don't need us to be vaccinated if we wanted to work, even part time." She saw the interest in my face, and said, "They're a great family to work for. I want to hire all my friends to work here with me. So will ya' do it?"

I lightly chuckled, knowing I had gotten myself into something here that was more than a Mother's Day tasting, and smiled saying, "Well if I am going to be selling wine, I better make sure I like it first." I took a sip of the aromatic lemon and honeysuckle and apricot, or was it nectarine, aroma in this wine. Mmmm, it was good. My eyebrows shot up and Betty said, "It's good huh? It's a Rhone style blend and it's always everyone's favorite white here. Jenn, I knew you were going to try it and going to love it."

I had tried grenache blanc and viogner at Stonefruit Cellars before, but I felt like I had closed that time in my life where I learned about wine. It really felt like the Covid Era was a natural end to my wine career. I felt like closing down the winery for Covid was a closing down of my career in wine too. But this wine and this experience of being the customer was doing something to me. Igniting the spark I had for wine. This picpul blanc had its pull on me, and it was bringing me back to wine sip by sip. You see, I had always wanted to learn about wine again but the restrictions on wineries were strict and enforced social distancing. So, there was a closing of the season's chapter, a closing of an experience for me as it wasn't personal. It felt very natural and normal as tasting rooms countywide had closed down production and tasting rooms. Some had opened again in Spring, namely ones with large backyards with tables and umbrellas like this that could pivot how their tasting room experience traditionally worked. This meant they could host seated outdoor tastings which were deemed healthier and safer than others which were strictly indoors.

There was so much so learn, and I was still so curious. They say that teachers are always students, and this felt so true to me. All because of this new-to-me varietal, I was helped to understand here were many things I didn't know about wine, and feeling the hopeful tug to learn more helped make me want to work at this winery. And hell, if Betty was into it, it must be good as she was discerning as all hell about her workplace environment. She preferred a place with no rules on her outfits and allowed her to make up the rules as she goes. She wasn't the type to ask permission from the manager above her for every special request a customer wanted. She would prefer to make up the policy and say it with conviction as if it was certainly true and something she knew as fact. I loved this confidence about her and tucked away a few characteristics, hoping they'd become part of my essence too.

When she came back around to check on us, she complimented my skills making such a pretty charcuterie board. She mentioned how the edible flowers were such a beautiful touch. She read my mind about trying another wine, and brought me a stemless glass with a bit of wine, perfectly sip sized. She said, "Jenn, you need to try this wine too. It's going to pair so well with that prosciutto! It's a sangiovese." I offered her some of our charcuterie board as she said it was beautiful. She complimented me again, "Jenn, you're always so creative, I missed you!"

I thanked her and sipped and thought to myself, damn, there are moments where Paso truly is a beautiful place full of beautiful people. They're renegades and don't have to follow the rules set forth by tradition and other wine regions like in Europe, but in this moment, the of "what grows together, grows together" is absolutely true. You see, the Italian style smoked ham prosciutto is exactly the kind of thing that grows in the same country as sangiovese grape varietals. Together, they're a real "chef's kiss" and delectable.

I felt like a renegade too. I had selected a path that was different, and yet made it work for me. I was inspired by my bold coworkers and the story of wine. I had tasted the good life and was taking it for myself. I was unsure I wanted to take on a part time job again, but my mom reminded me how I was the highest tip earner at Stonefruit Canyon, and I could likely do that again here. It's said that, "The degree to which a person can grow is directly proportional to the amount of truth they can accept about themselves without running away." I knew I needed to learn more about wine to truly understand it. I also knew I needed to make money. I remembered the Forbes training which taught us this industry doesn't have an earnings cap on it, and I could be in charge of my own pay — because of tips and commissions. I wanted to grow as I was willing to understand I had to work for it. With all that going for this job, I couldn't say no, and told Betty I could work weekends only, because it was on weekends that my son's dad and I had organized in our co-parenting plan that he would be in the care of his dad. During the week I would be busy homeschooling and caring for my son, so on weekends I could work at the winery. My new life was falling just into place.

FRIENDS

A few weekends after I started working at Celestial Cellars, Betty was making her wishes to hire friends was coming true. As the wineries re-opened more and more, they needed more hands-on deck to help our eager and thirsty customers.

I came in to work one day, in my usual peppy way and said, "Good morning, Party People!" Betty turned to me from the blue wingback chair in the tasting room and said, "Jenn, guess who I just hired?! He starts next week!" This time when working with Berry, I noticed she had changed a bit too. Nowadays use usually spoke with interrobangs following her sentences. Her enthusiasm was contagious. It felt like we were best friends who were assigned different teachers but got to recess together.

I smiled, happy for her. She hired her second friend, and apparently, he was a former coworker to work with us. I thought it was cool she was moving fast to make her dream work environment come true. Typical Betty. I did however wonder to myself if she noticed that she gave me a hint when she said, "*He* starts next week." Then I daydreamed and I questioned myself who I'd want the new male hire to be. After a pause, I hopefully questioned, "Josh?" And she stood up, tapped my shoulder, smiled and said, "You're right!" We were all in for a treat this summer.

TEA TREK

My parents and peer friendships became very important to me during this era. I was a newly single mom with a five-year-old son; everyone really pulled through to help me emotionally. They encouraged me and Luna to go on walks around Atascadero Lake. They also came over to help me decorate my new apartment up in the mountains. I wandered around TJ Maxx until they began to close. I found my little deck area under a wise oak tree was the perfect place for me to roll out a yoga mat.

My friend Emery joined me for a Tea Trek, a hiking and tea drinking club I had started in efforts to go try new trails and try a variety of tea varietals with friends. On one particularly memorable hike she was the only one who came. Everyone was too busy, or still afraid of Covid germs to go outside and hike. We stopped at a concrete bench at Atascadero Lake Park to rest out feet, our fitness endurance really took a hit when he stopped going to the gym together. I poured our tea I had brewed for the trek. It was a Yerba Mate, and I selected it as it's said to bring the one who brews it energy and good vibes. Emery asked how I liked my job at the tasting room. I told her it's an interesting education experience when I worked in the tasting room. I was getting to be a student of wine myself, as I was constantly learning. I also was a teacher, imparting wine knowledge and educating customers who came to the tasting room. There was a lot to learn, and teach. Both sides of it was a fulfilling process. I quickly learned that wine is sexy and I liked talking to grown-

ups again. Grown-ups who looked at me as a source of knowledge and education. I felt good knowing things they wanted to
know. My personal fulfillment bucket was getting drops and
drops of attention and enjoyment. People gave me attention.
People tipped me money, among other unique gifts. I was given
free wine to drink in the name of education. I worked with interesting people. I was in a beautiful environment. I began to learn I
was capable at being a whole woman and appreciated for things I
did. It has been a long time since that happened. These long-lost
feelings of appreciation are familiar to people who are over-
worked and overexerted. Learning something new also has the
tendency to invigorate. A self-proclaimed life-long learner, I
thrived by learning something new and being good at it. This job
began with half days on Friday and Monday and full days on
Saturday and Sunday. That's 24 per week where break times are
built in, and there's uninterrupted bathroom breaks. To a busy
mom, that's the biggest promotion! The hardest thing about these
bathroom breaks was the fact I had to remind myself to call them
by their proper grown up and mature term, "bathroom break"
versus "potty time" as those parenting toddlers at home are
embarrassingly apt to say.

As I was pouring hot tea from the largest insulated water
bottle and into the tea cups I brought, she brought up how Adrian
had just visited her family earlier that weekend. She gushed that
she had enjoyed that I sold him so much wine as she got to enjoy
a few cases that he gifted her. She said she may have drank too
much of the cabernet, as it was her favorite. She then mentioned
that Adrian doesn't have a girlfriend and she wondered if I knew
anyone who would be interested in dating him. After just a
moment of contemplation, I smiled looked into her big brown
eyes and said, "I think I would be." She smiled and said, "Ok, so
I guess I'll just give him your number then?!" I nodded yes, and
we sipped the tea before continuing our Tea Trek.

LAST ONE

Summer is when the grapevine's leaves grow and grow. These leaves work as little green solar panels powering the grapes' germination and growth. This allows for the grapes' growth and then when it's a hot weather day, the grapes ripen. The heat encourages sugar in the juice to form, and this is where the alcohol comes from. High sugar makes for a high alcohol content. All because of sunlight, isn't that absolutely wild? I was always impressed.

This summer brought up an interesting point about wine pricing. Winemakers make a certain amount of wine given the allotment of grapes they grew. Not having an exact number of how many grape clusters will actually grow, the wine makers can't exactly predict how much wine their vineyard will yield. It all depends on the sun. One cluster makes one glass of wine. So, four clusters have to ripen to make one bottle of wine. That's a lot of sun!

However, nature does what it wants, and the sunshine changes year to year. Even after making something from the plump ripe grapes, winemakers also can't predict how much of the wine will be sold. It's a product like any other, and they're at the mercy of how well the wine is received by those who taste it. It can be sampled fresh in the tasting room by those visiting the tasting room and sold on the website in online sales. There's also the factor of whether or not a winery distributes wine across the world, and what opportunities they get for themselves at restaurants as well. All this means is that at one point in time, there's a big possibility of one case of a wine left for sale in the tasting room cellar.

There's a vastly different philosophy on how to handle this case. At Stonefruit Canyon, when there was one case left, we advertised this with verbiage like this "ONLY one precious case left. You know you love it, so buy it BEFORE WE COMPLETLEY sell out" and the dust on the bottle only makes it more precious as it's thought of as a rare find from the back of the cellar. The idea of it being around for a while made the owners think the bottles are all accounted for. Perhaps already drank, or in some collector's cellar waiting for the right moment. This pricing model also accounted for those who read articles from sources like Wine Enthusiast or travel bloggers, or even wine writers. As time went on, the bottles are only more precious as they have been described and advertised by that many more people that time provides.

Alternatively, at Celestial Cellars, when we had one case left, I was trained to discount it to make room for the next vintage, or year of wine. This discount would be somewhere between 30-60% off with the verbiage on the sign of, "Help us clear out and prepare for the next vintage release." Meaning, for example, the malbec from the most recent harvest of wine was just recently bottled and ready to be sold, and that the malbec from previous years vintage was taking up the space needed for the new vintage. This is from the headspace that the new wine is even more important than this lonely case. The excitement for the new release overpowered the reverence for the previous release.

In both cases it was a matter of having space for the next vintage release, but it truly boggled me that the last case could be thought of so vastly differently. It was a difference in philosophy for sure. Neither is wrong or right, they're just different. The two wineries were alike in so many ways, and they really were only miles from each other geographically. On a quest to understand things, this pricing difference revealed that there's really not one way of handling the same tasting room occurrence even with two family-run wineries. This is where the differences in tasting room procedures really is apparent. There are many sorts of things can vary from winery to winery. I wondered if this is relatable to relationships. If someone is always available that might make them more desirable, but to another, the excess availability may feel like a burden you have to entertain. It was interesting to see how things like wine, and people's time, really is subjective.

CONSTELLATION

To add to the mix of people I've met at the winery, I fell in love fast with the winery cat named Milky Way. He's a large and in charge floofy orange cat. Named after the Milky Way constellation of stars in the galaxy that actually looks like a connect-the-dot-cat, he is a flirty cat who loves laying in the middle of your table, or on the couch cushion next to you. He's such a friendly lion, and has been known to be thankful for a bite of cheese, although he is amply fed by the tasting room staff, and a vineyard mouse or lizard here and there.

Celestial Cellars, a family-owned winery in Paso Robles, had been in business for nearly 30 years. Founded in 1995 by the Bergheart Family, like many who have been around for a while, the winery has grown from the ground up while maintaining its focus on winemaking and vineyard management. Second-generation owner and Director of Winemaking Mr. Bergheart said the journey has required long hours and a commitment to quality. "Winemaking isn't just about the finished bottle — it's about the labor, the land, and the decisions you make every single day," Mr. Bergheart said and then a second later added, "It's pruning in the winter, walking the vineyard in the summer heat, making the call on when to pick. It's being covered in grape skins at 2AM, exhausted but pushing through because you know the work you put in now is what makes the wine worth drinking later. Celestial Cellars was never a vanity project. It was, and still is, about getting our hands dirty, making honest wines, and building something that lasts." His experience paired with the no rules aspect of Paso which meant that we could be overeducated or undereducated and it didn't matter whatsoever. It wasn't until a year after working in the industry for all this time, that I'd even learned of what a WSET was and how people could prove their knowledge and experience in this. The WSET stands for Wine and Spirits Education Trust, and it's a company that tests people on their wine skills. People study for the test through a certified school, like Napa Valley Wine Academy or Central Coast School of Wine. It was when my coworker Jocelyn left her desk as wine club manager to pour wine on a busy Saturday that I learned about her taking the first three level tests through WSET. She now introduced herself as a Sommelier. During the shift, I wrote a note to myself with the letters WSET on it, and stuck it in my back left pocket with my cash tips to make sure I remembered to Google it when I got home.

Before learning about the serious education side of wine, it, seemed a bit pretentious. It, at first glance, appears to be a bunch of people with flowery language, making up descriptors like marketing majors who spin shit into chocolate. But there was, in fact, more to it, I had learned. There was so much that was there all along, if you really looked for the truth in it.

Inspired to learn the truth, I learned from my coworker Jocelyn, that when you smell the wine, yes it may have a scent like a grape, but we weren't going to call it that. We were going to call it an olallieberry and black currant and even ripe strawberry, to be simple about it. We were going to be very very specific. We knew what we were selling. We were selling the tradition of Europe's old-world wines, but making them new world. This meant it was winemaking done in a renegade way where we could play with the flavors and blends. Jocelyn said that the ability to describe scent and flavor is what she learned when she earned her Level 1 WSET certificate, and that she learned about different wine regions and how weather and soil effects the grape's juice in Level 2 courses. She nerded out a bit more, and learned how to read wine labels, and learn more about wine regions around the world in her Level 3 certification class. I loved being around someone who also pursued knowledge outside of work that helped her shifts be rich in meaning. She wasn't just working at a winery; it was truly a lifestyle to her.

During our shifts together, we would talk food. She was a big foodie. We would talk about our week's meal prep, and what we would pair our food, and exchange pictures of dishes we made. In the afternoons, between customers, or in the mornings before customers flooded in, we would talk about all what wine would you pair with this meal. We would kind of joke about how there's a wine for every dish and there's even a wine that goes with McDonald's food. That's right, we believe there's a wine for the highest Michelin star serving of Wagyu beef, or medallion of filet mignon and that would be an aged cabernet sauvignon. Also, that there's even a wine that pairs with McDonald's French fries — champagne. The most challenging meal we thought of pairing wine with was Taco Bell, but settled on a merlot for the spicy finish, which is wine speak for aftertaste.

There's a wine for every occasion, for every happy highlight, for every sad sorrow. There's a wine for every emotion and feeling and celebration. After learning the lingo of wine, if there wasn't a food for it, we could talk about similar things though that we could be making it up in a believable way as there was an element of personal preference, not just fact, involved.

It really came down to the fact that it was our own gumption to get beyond the sale and pair the wine with your personality with what you wanted in a beverage. That's what being a "wine expert" did to us sometimes — it made wine enjoyment and education fun. We all wanted to help you find something to fall in love with. Sometimes that love lasted as long as the bottle did. For others, it was for a lifetime.

REUNITED

B etty needed reliable staff for the tasting room, and as the manager she was responsible for things like that. So, she continued to reach out to those who she knew from previous jobs. After she hired Josh from another winery, she hired Sharon who was working at yet another Westside winery. The only person she didn't directly hire for the tasting room, was Jocelyn who came with Celestial Cellars as their wine club manager but she was great fit for this growing team. It was wild to think of part of the crew coming back together. So much had happened in the world, but some constants remained. After going through the Covid era and coming through to the other side, masks and vaccinations and all, we all were a bit different, but there was some familiarity as well. The nostalgic familiarly of saying, "Good morning Party People" when entering the tasting room for my shift must have sounded like familiar bells to Josh and Betty. The wine world is Paso is vast, but truly feels small at times. I couldn't have predicted any of this on my 2021 bingo card.

One Sunday during the Summer Concert Series at Celestial Cellars, Josh's grandfather came to the event and greeted me with a hug upon initial meeting. This act of instant physical touch inspired me to say, "Oh now I know where Josh gets his flirty nature from...it's genetic!"

His family took a seat on the plush outdoor furniture in the backyard at the winery, where the tunes and wine were flowing on that Sunday afternoon just as it was every other day. They ordered a bottle of cabernet sauvignon to share and dined on food from the food truck which was slinging arguably the best food truck tacos on the Central Coast. It seems Josh's family has the same impeccable taste and preference in spending an afternoon in the sunshine while eating Mexican food and drinking a fine cab makes for a happy Sunday indeed.

YOU CAN'T FROSÉ ALL DAY IF YOU DON'T START IN THE MORNING

When Betty was coming up with the recipe for the frosé, which is a frozen rosé slushy type drink, at Celestial Cellars her ultimate goal was to make a frosé (pronounced "froze eh?" like it's a question) that was refreshing and deceptively boozy. Deceptively as it could contain rosé wine but she didn't want it to taste heavily sugared or be too alcoholic. Basically, the goal was light and refreshing. She rented a Margarita Man machine locally and researched different ratios of the premade mix that gives it a slushy consistency but doesn't actually freeze entirely when refrigerated. She made some too light which had not much color and lacked the rosé quality. So, it was an effort for all the senses not just taste. It had to smell right and look right too. It also had to be cold, but not frozen solid. This kept Betty busy, but luckily, she had lots of friends who were willing to help her test out the mixture ratios. They also imbibed at other establishments to do the most delicious of research.

As the countdown for summertime was nearing, Betty set to work coming up with the perfect ratio of rosé wine and slushy mix to make a frosé. It needed to be perfectly remarkably refreshing on a hot summer day. Now the origin of the term frosé is up for debate in the industry, but the related term "Rosé all Day", was originally coined by the owner of a nearby restaurant called, Celsius. The owner claims to have she invented the phrase "rosé all day" and interestingly enough, Betty used to work there before working at Stonefruit Canyon which proves just how small town the Paso area is.

Mixing the wine and ice and frosé mix was a fun science experiment of sorts as Betty and her friends were the guinea pigs trying the attempts at frosé perfection. After a few batches, she knew she'd perfected it when Josh asked, "Are you sure there's alcohol in this?" Having a drink that's the perfect blend of flavors without alcohol overpowering it is definitely the desired outcome. When Betty confirmed there was in fact two bottles of rosé mixed in, Josh's soulful eyes got bigger and said, "This could be dangerous." It wouldn't be the thick of the warm weather tourist season for another three months so it was a good time to continue perfecting a drink that was as refreshing and mild-tasting as frosé is.

SOME PEOPLE DON'T CHANGE

Being the flirty natured young man he is, there was always some sort of flirty tension between some female customers and other coworkers with Josh. My crush was long gone, and I liked seeing how things played out with Josh nowadays. Josh was still was very good looking, still was a close talker which made many things he said feel like they were spoken just for you. This did things to women when they drank wine. While some of the tension was more palpable than others, it was mostly all in good heart. But honestly, I started seeing him in a new light.

Sometimes his attraction would cause others around him to act wild. Things would sway to the more disruptive when women couldn't control themselves around him. At times it was a bit loud, and learning towards sometimes inappropriate. When it was disruptive, it irked the flow at Celestial Cellars in a way that made me count the minutes until my shift was over. Sharon needed extra Xanax on days they worked together in the tasting room. One time, we had a coworker who was chaos in a bottle. Arriving late was one thing, but the way she'd mix sugar free Red Bulls with the port wine was next level. She would make out with her guy "friends" who visited on days her boyfriend didn't visit and still claimed they were all just friends. She even showed up to work on a day that she wasn't scheduled to and when confronted about it, she refused to leave. She waited out her shift in the backroom and worked on her community college homework while clocked in. I personally can't believe this was allowed, but I can only assume that confrontation would have cost the company more than simply paying her for six hours of work.

That kind of chaos made no sense to me. Josh made sense. Josh had his posse of followers. They ranged from 21 up to mid-40's. I couldn't blame any of them. I had seen it too. His personality was just like wine. Definitely composed of the right blend. He was tart like the outer layer of and sweet on the inside like those Sour Patch Kids gummy candies. He was wise like a wine that had been in the bottle for a decade less than me and yet aging to perfection. He was also accessible to all like a merlot. He was rare and lovable as a German riesling — a light and refreshing drink on a hot summer day.

SAYING NO

J osh and Betty both talked about getting food on their lunch break. They could talk about what they could order and what would be a delicious option for when the time came. These foodies loved talking about food, and being around food, but didn't actually get around to eating it. Many times, their long-awaited food remained half eaten on the counter in the kitchen. I wondered if they didn't want to stop their buzz, or they liked talking about food more than eating it.

We often get people we know bringing us food to the tasting room. We had some staff changes, and Jocelyn, our old wine club manager and current wine educator, has her roommate bring empanadas. Betty's family member brought homemade bagel bread to the tasting room. Betty thought it was very nice but no one ate any of it. This happened with a caterer who specialized in hot dogs, too. No one wanted to eat the hot dogs from the food truck at the event. Kind of strange how these two were so good about saying "no" to food. This willpower impressed me as I wasn't similar to them in this way.

The two of them showed their restraint, and Josh especially surprised me. In an afternoon on the weekend shift, Josh was talking to the girl who he knew. She was a long-time customer and was like Nina in that she was also a Bringer, bringing her friends everywhere with her. I had taken note of her as I was working the door at these events which happened weekly on Sundays, so I had gotten to know the regulars. I noticed a ring on her left ring finger. I couldn't believe she was flirting with Josh so hard, and wondered why her husband was never with her at the winery. For weeks Josh said she was single as he'd been to her house and it was definitely a woman's house. But one day, he wasn't as excited to see her pop into the tasting room. He told me that the night before he just figured it out something about her and he was disappointed. He said he saw her putting her wedding ring back on after they hooked up. He expressed disdain that she lied and was ignoring her texts. When she then showed up at his work, week after week and saying she's too drunk to drive and was wanting a ride home, Josh turned to me and said that he loves "getting laid, but it's not worth the DUI."

I noticed how he said "it's not worth" versus "she's not worth" and felt like this era wasn't over for Josh for it was the proximity to her that mattered over who she was herself. The quote that continues to justify tomfoolery is one by Otto Van Bismark, who said, "God protects the drunks and fools or is it fools and drugs?" He coined that quote and it stands as a humorous way of suggesting that sometimes people who make risky or unwise decisions seem to get away with it unscathed. But it seemed Josh knew when it was time to just say "no."

FIRST DATE

A drian knew a few things about me before ever going out with me. He observed that I didn't go out late with coworkers and he knew I took motherhood very seriously. He used this knowledge to plan our dates. He started with something I was comfortable with already. I knew Emery and Aaron, and their two boys, so he invited me to meet them at their house. Aaron was going to make his specialty, white chili. I had never tried that before and was curious. Emery told me she planned to make a gluten and dairy free cake. I was skeptical of that at first, but after one bite I learned to always trust her kitchen concoctions. They were practicing a dry January, so I didn't bring wine for a hostess gift this time. Being at their house without my own son was hard. Her boys asked me where my son was, as they're used to playing together when they see me. Plus, seeing them really made me miss my son even more. The boys were running up and down their home's hallway, and my son wasn't the third in the pack, as usual. I felt awkward and checked my phone a lot. I was checking if my son's dad was texting me about our son or something as I knew they were getting used to living without me on weekends. Our co-parenting arrangement was aided by many books, the Instagram account, @themichellemultak of the Moving On Method and copious Reddit threads about family separations. Their advice was sage and right what I needed. However, this wasn't talked about in the books, posts or threads. I felt so ill-prepared for seeing my son's friends but not my son too. The books talked about keeping busy doing things you love to do, and forgot you love to do, when you're not with your kids. Nothing mentioned doing familiar things without your child.

I tried to focus on who I was with though. I enjoyed their backyard's fire feature surrounded by cozy seating. I enjoyed the company of Emery and observed how Adrian read bedtime books to their boys. He sat on the floor next to their beds and read a book called, 5-Minute Star Wars Bedtime Stories. It never lasted five minutes though because he'd read a few in a row. I also observed how Aaron and Adrian kind of teased each other, in the way close male friendships I saw in buddy movies on TV. I saw how he was the true to himself at the winery and with his friends. He was the same person. His heart overflows with love and is helpful by nature. He was talking about his job with Aaron, and when us girls chimed in and asked what he meant by something, he didn't talk down to us. I liked that.

As a new cat person, he told me about his two long-haired cats. One was a Maine Coon named Mayo who actually came from a cattery in Maine. I asked what a cattery is and learned they are pet sanctuaries/stores for cats. His second cat is part Maine Coon and named Mojo Jojo, but goes by Mojo for short. Mayo and Mojo's images took up 95% of his camera roll. He showed me countless pictures of them since their kittenhood. I never imaged that I, a woman who purposefully adopted a hypoallergenic dog was dating a man who two long hair cats. I didn't know it at the time, but my allergies would never be the same.

Cats have a slow love. They don't love everyone they meet on a walk, like my dog did. Cats observe and then tolerate affection for a moment. They love on their own terms and fall slowly for the treats you share before they ever fall in love with a human. I think they'd healed my people pleaser nature. They taught me to sit back, relax, and wait for the right person to come pet me. It was action from a different perspective, and I felt this style was healthier for me.

RIDE SHARE

When coming to Paso, think about if you would like to have a chauffeur drive you around. This wouldn't be about being fancy as much as it is safety and convenience, and yes Uber and Lyft count as chauffeur, and I am still unsure why people don't think of ride shares as that quite yet. I love to tell my customers, "It would free up your worry about imbibing too much, and also relieve worry about the often tiny-labeled roads around here. Tour services can drive your own car, or drive you around in a logo-marked bus or limo. Most of them will have you pick if you want to stay on the west side or the east side, depending on what you want or where you want to go. If thinking about wanting to try a new winery but also check out some old favorites in which you are a member, you also might need to tell your driver what wineries you've already been to and the new ones you want to check out so they can add that to the list. It should be fully customizable.

Betty overhears me and adds to this conversation as the bar inside Celestial Cellars is in the middle of the tasting room and less private than when the customers are seated at a table outside. The customers actually benefit from this, and personally it reminds me of Stonefruit Cellars where a busy bar can lead you to hearing comments from all of us working there on Sunday morning. Betty adds, in the assertive yet approachable way she speaks, "Don't forget to tip your driver, and even if you choose the all-inclusive option where it pays for your tastings at the winery either buy bottles and/or tip your server there too. Often times the people working at the winery love the tours a little less because people are more drunk and forget kindness," Betty adds. "Not that everyone would do that, but it happens." By now Josh is done with his restocking work and joins in the conversation and says, "You gals talk about food yet? I recommend you also add a stop for lunch or plan ahead for dinner to make sure you get a table. Some tours include lunch from a place called Take-away Deli that's delicious. Or even Breezway Bistro. We love them. But you absolutely cannot rely on Uber or Lyft, as many of the wineries are in a no cell service range so you won't even be able to organize a pick up." Sharon joins in and says that, "There's lots on The Square in Paso too. I like Irish Wish for fresh food with great beers and cocktails. Or Grande Cucina for Italian food and especially for desserts as Italian's do dessert best. The Little Rugrats, or simply TLR as it's called by locals, is the place for amazing French food and wine galore."

Enjoying the community vibe the tasting room has right now, it feels like we're all reunited at Stonefruit Canyon. I want to add more to the conversation, and say to my customers with eye contact, "As you can see, this town loves its food and is gifted with close proximity to the ocean for seafood, meadows for beef and boar and gifted with proximity to vineyards for wine."

UNDERCOVER BOSS

To gear up for the next season, the winery needed to hire a few more eager hands willing to put in the work in 100-degree summer months. The lure of wine industry discount and hearing live music while at work lured in a few fun characters and we soon had a few new people on board. One of the most interesting was Lisa, a New Jersey transplant who moved here with dreams of opening up her own wine bar. She had taken her day job online, so she could work in the evenings after working at the tasting room during the day. She seemed promising as her passion for wine spoke loud when first meeting her. This crumbled fast as Lisa said she also applied to work at BevMo. She wowed Betty enough during the interview and began working midweek before joining us for a busy weekend. She couldn't keep up with even the slowest of days. The iPad system was toughest for her so much so that I wondered what New Jersey was really like. I jest. It just seemed too far off from reality of her being a woman who applied to this job digitally, meaning that she had to work a computer enough to apply, and now she couldn't do the job here whatsoever. It almost felt like we were on that TV show, "Undercover Boss" and being tested time and time again. But in reality, she just sucked at this iPad interface system we used. When Josh served her a sample of the our Rhone style blend of white wine to try, she said, "It's called Bella! Like my favorite Disney princess Belle. I'll love it!"

She also couldn't do cellar work, or read the tasting menu without having 10,000 questions. She was asked to leave the winery after one particularly bad shift where she couldn't be left alone to do her job for even one minute despite months of training. Betty couldn't wait to tell me she ran into her at BevMo a month later, but besides saying "hi" to each other, they didn't interact as Lisa wasn't working the register or even stocking shelves. To this day we don't know what she was doing working there. She's one of those people who passed through the winery, and you wish you followed them on social media so you could see where they landed and ended up later.

LADIES MAN

I t's important to bring up there was in fact a male working there besides Josh, as it did feel pretty woman heavy at times. There was also Matt, who was likely hoping for some of that attention Josh got a lot of. He spoke a lot about his home life, and said he was married and had three girls at home. He wanted this in-person job to compliment his online marketing job which was just part time. I related to that notion of wanting to better one's self and socialize with grown up adults at work. His personality at home helped him fit in, and then hindered him at Celestial Cellars, unfortunately. You see, not only was he a girl magnet at home, he was a girl magnet at work too. He enjoyed this attention for whatever masculine nature you want to quote. But basically, he seemed desperate to connect with someone in more than a parenting role. This was so apparent to women at the tasting room. I would have voted him Most Likely to Have a Tasting Room Affair if that was a thing. I was a people-pleaser myself and could notice his attachment style in an instant. He was serving compliments at work and three meals a day at home. Serving everyone but himself. Come to think of it, perhaps he was on a journey of saving himself too? Perhaps he was acting out of bravery, in respect to Brene Brown's quote, "The broken hearted are the bravest among us, they dare to love." Whatever it was, it didn't last too long but at least he had some fun before his time with us at the winery ended.

ATTENTION PLEASE

Wine is civilized but whining is not. Neither is whistling to get attention. Getting a wine educator's attention is simple. Eye contact paired with an empty glass will usually do the trick. Please order after, not before, being acknowledged with eye contact or a verbal "hello" or "hi" so we clearly hear your request. There's nothing as mood-killing as having to repeat yourself or not being heard.

If you approach one of us workers before getting eye contact, you may face the awkwardness as when one of the newbies Ryan, was approached by a customer. He was walking to the kitchen area, which doubled as a work area for dishes and trays, when he was approached by a customer. He replied, "Well, I'm on break, but I can take care of you. How can I help?"

And it was weird because the customer's request wasn't simple — they wanted to switch out the bottles of wine coming to them in their wine club shipment. This sort of thing was better suited to Sharon, or Josh, so while Ryan started to help them, the customer actually had to repeat all the requests to Josh again, as he wanted Josh to handle this instead. Having to repeat oneself and wait is pretty lame for the customer to experience in this aspirational high-end environment. It really would have been streamlined, and much more elegant, if the customer sought out someone equipped with more time to handle the request. Eye contact would have spoken that he was indeed available to assist the customer.

SECOND, AND THIRD DATES

O nce in a blue moon, I was more comfortable staying out late as I wasn't missing time with my son as he was asleep at his dad's house. I didn't have to stare at my phone, worrying they'd call because they couldn't find the Band-Aids or something. Now, I understand that grabbing a drink together is more than a hydrating beverage, but an unspoken reason to connect. I mostly preferred small get togethers. It was one-on-one's that really brought me joy. I could really connect and get to know someone better that way. I wasn't distracted by the others in the group, waitstaff, or other patrons. Having quality time with someone felt so special to me.

Adrian used this information about me when planning our other dates. Our first alone date, aka official first date without our mutual friends was Main St. Grill, a steakhouse in Templeton. We met up there and because his car is very recognizable, I saw him get out of his car holding a bouquet of flowers. He had remembered that I love fresh flowers and that my dad's parents were florists before WWII. They were beautiful and laid on the table next to us at dinner. Adrian ordered a ribeye steak, and I the filet mignon. As we both ordered red meat, I suggested we get a glass of red wine. He said with enthusiasm, "Jenn, that's up to you! You totally know more than me. You should pick," as he handed me the wine list. I skimmed the list while imagining the map of tasting rooms we had at the bar, and where these wines were located. I remembered learning how wine from warmer climates tend to have a bolder flavor and higher alcohol. I like flavor, but didn't want to feel tipsy, so I picked a wine from the Westside of Paso as it would have cooler nights and likely less alcohol. I selected a zinfandel from a winery just west of the tasting room where we met. It should be similar to the ones at Stonefuit Canyon as they're both from the Templeton Gap AVA, but this one may have vineyards in the Willow Creek AVA or Adelaida AVA. I thought it was a great opportunity to try a wine together, for the first time. He was typically my customer, and I poured for him, so having someone else pour for us really changed the mood. The waiter showed us the bottle, and went to pour a little sip for Adrian, but he said, "Oh no, please have her taste it first, she's the wine expert here!" I blushed and felt I had to put myself to the test. I gently grabbed my glasses stem, brought the goblet to my nose, inhaled, gently sipped and smiled as I rested the glass back on the table. I told the waiter, "Seems like I made a good choice. We will enjoy that together." The waiter proceeded to pour a good amount of wine into Adrian's glass and then mine. I felt so good inside. Here we were sharing wine together. We were even seated next to each other in the booth all romantically at the restaurant.

But what I didn't see coming was the blush on Adrian's face, when I then told the waiter, "It's good you're leaving the bottle at the table, I know this man, and he is very, very thirsty." The waiter smiled, a coy knowing smile, and I asked Adiran, "Um, what did I say wrong? You're blushing, and he thinks I'm onto something." Adrian, leaned closer to my ear and said, "When you say someone's 'thirsty' it means they're horny, Jenn."

"It does not, Adrian, no way! I say it all the time when describing customers. I've called another regular in the tasting room, Tony, thirsty. I say Josh is thirsty all the time."

"Well, Jenn, I don't know what to tell you, but it's true. Google it." I didn't want to take out my phone at this fancy restaurant, so I just trusted him. But boy oh boy, did I have some regrets as I recounted the times and ways in which I apparently outed people as being amorous. Maybe, unknowingly I was a wingman for Josh or Tony. Maybe I made them blush too. This was the kind of growing pain I expected early on in my wine career, not later in it. Clearly, there was so much to learn about wine, and the words used to describe it, and other adult things.

I KNOW THE OWNER

C elestial Cellars is family owned and it seems that when someone in your family owns a winery, that's the place the family hangout. Some of their names are even on the bottle, if the wine is named after them. It makes for fun parties in the backyard, and shifts with familiar faces. It's great working for a family-run place like this as these familiar faces are friendly and genuinely thankful that you're there working for them. I imagine it's like meeting your fan club members, because we all have to like the area and wine in order to work there.

Another way to make these types of relationship is through these ever-so-popular wine cruises. Basically, you get to travel to Europe's wineries and river cruises with the owner of the winery in Paso. This is how wine club members really get immersed in the winery. They love going on them, and getting all buddy-buddy with someone who owns a winery. For us tasting room staff, this is kind of odd. You see, we earn a commission for every wine club we sign up. It's usually a $10 commission. But when we sign people up for these travel trips, there's no commission. I connected to these customers who signed up for the winery club, and the trip but there is not a financial benefit for us when doing this. I wish I understood the back end of this decision and new trend. Does the owner travel for free if enough people sign up for the trip? I wish I knew more, but the separation between staff and inner workings of these trips leaves me so curious.

I do know that these experiences connect and bond owner

and customer and are charming and all, but it leads to awkward-ness when people try to take advantage of the perks that aren't actually meant for them. We had someone come in and ask for the owner, saying they were his cousin and did a cruise trip with him too. Information about the winery family is searchable on Google so it's not actually a hard thing to lie about. But, as the tasting went on, Sharon shared about the wine one by one, noting the awards it has won, and what foods to best pair with it. Their connection to the family only came at the end when they asked for "the family discount." It was when they didn't ask if anyone from the family was there, and didn't want to make a phone call, or even leave a note. Sharon suspected they may not truly have been family at all. But I overheard the family discount request from them again, "Hey, come on, I know the owner!," said with some flippant confidence all for a discount on their wine tasting. They must have known not to push and take advantage of their pseudo-connection and buy bottles, they merely wanted part of their tasting fees, which were $20 each, covered. So, the ever-smart and full of decorum Sharon, wanting to avoid confronta-tion, gave them 10% off, and reminded them that they could call the family when they wanted a larger discount on the purchase of bottles or cases. All that to save a mere $4. Oof, people were creative to save a couple bucks.

ON ONE KNEE

F alling for Adrian was easy. I knew I liked how I felt with him when I felt comfortable singing my go-to karaoke song, Weird Al's Amish Paradise. It came on the radio as he had it as part of an Apple Play playlist connected to his phone. I was singing along singing, "Churning lots of butter, raise a barn on Monday, soon I'll raise another" when I look over and see what set my heart into a flutter! Adrian knew the obscure lyrics too and was singing along with me. I was being my quirky self, and he was being quirky with me.

The first few dates you share with someone really show you who you are as you're talking about yourself a lot. I learned I liked myself when I was with Adrian. I could be a mom obsessed with her son and he'd ask questions about our life and routine. Specific questions like what I was teaching in homeschool this week, or what friends we were visiting this week. He asked what kind of toys my son played with, and happened to know about the characters and toys, too, as he'd bought them as Christmas gifts for Aaron and Emery's kids before.

Not only do you learn about yourself on dates, you're also asking questions which reveal what you care about, too. Because I was so close to my parents, I asked about his relationship with his. He shared how his mom loves Jimmy Buffet songs and eating seafood. He told me a story about her eating a 5-pound lobster at a restaurant when she visited last, and how proud he was of her. I heard he was proud of a woman for eating, and I knew then that he'd never food shame me. He told me how his mom visits a few times a year and that they love taking road trips to National Parks. I knew right then I wouldn't have to drag him on a hike with me, and would likely get to be a passenger on a road trip. He mentioned how his spiritual counselor dad lives in Georgia and has a quintessential Georgia Peach wife. I love southern food and hoped to visit one day and get to know them over a glass of sweet tea.

I didn't doubt my worth around him. He encouraged me to shine and to grow. After this, things moved fast. His official proposal included a few tears. Mostly his, not mine, and a platinum set peach sapphire. He picked out platinum as it's the strongest metal and peach sapphire to represent our meeting place, Stonefruit Canyon. Despite our short time dating, our mutual friendships spoke volumes and we bonded over wishing we'd have met decades ago. But, alas, he was living and working under the sea in a submarine, and I'd hardly even stick my face underwater in a pool. It's no wonder we didn't meet sooner. We had to make the most out of the time we had together. Since we both saw ourselves as family-oriented people, we knew we just clicked in place. I never imagined my job in customer service would get me a marriage proposal from a really great guy. It felt as though it's true, when you do what you love, your life follows. I love learning, and that's how I met the love of my life.

FAMILY GATHERING

S ticking to the story of family gatherings, oftentimes generous family members bring wine to dinners, parties, and other get togethers. When people share Paso wine, it's often just the beloved family with whom you share a choice bottle with. I have learned that for the best experience for your taste buds, open these exquisite bottles first, and save the Trader Joes wine for last when our taste buds are burnt out from the wines and flavorful food before it.

Speaking of family, one afternoon Josh was helping his customers and one from his group was on the second tasting, the chardonnay. They brought up the story of really wanting to get to the reds to find out which wine it was that their boyfriend's aunt's friend had poured for them that one time. This is a pretty vague request to us in the tasting room because there's so much change in the harvest year after year, and we produced so many red wines. The grapes grow in different weather conditions and may yield more or less juice depending on the amount of rain that year and the complex interplay of geology, soil, climate, and culture. Even if they knew the exact grape in that wine they loved, it may taste different this vintage. Plus, we all know what you pair the final product with is one of the final parts of the flavor equation. Maybe the aunt had the wine chilled or perhaps stored improperly. Maybe the aunt was devious and poured a wine from a box into a bottle. So, when trying to take a customer's description of something she drank once thanks to her generous boyfriend's aunt, it's really difficult to find out which one it was when the description is short and sweet like, "It was a red wine from here," or even if they describe it being, "In a really pretty bottle" we're going to need more info than that.

The closest way I can describe this is like when we would go to a record store in the 1990's hoping to find the album for a song you heard on the radio. All the humming the tune, and singing the lyrics at the worker sometimes wouldn't be enough to help the store worker help you. Even if the worker listened to the same radio station as you, people's pitch and interpretation of lyrics is really up to the imagination. This is the same as wine. Although where I imagine the record store worker got a kick out of hearing you hum the song time and time again. We really wish we did know what that one wine that you loved that one time was.

WINK WINK

I t was early in the day and Sharon was nearby and pouring for a group of male customers at a table right outside the tasting room doors. They shared that they were in town for their friend's bachelor party, and they had rented an AirBnB for the weekend. Some wanted to golf and some wanted to go wine tasting, so the group spread across Paso for the day. The men were normal enough and gave frat boy vibes with their worn in Rainbow brand leather sandals, their collars popped on pastel Polo shirts. But I quickly noticed that one man in particular seemed to me like he was checking out Sharon's body in the most non-covert way possible. Her babydoll dress wasn't even that short, but you could tell he thought it was just right. As Sharon was pouring him the tannat, he said directly to her, "This time, make it stiff" and winked. Even I blushed for her! It's not like that's how it even worked. In the tasting room we have no control over the alcohol in the wine like they do at bars.

But like most these men didn't think of that. They were out wine tasting but one was doing something different with his tongue — speaking in double entendre. Being the happily married and calm chick she is, she didn't skip a beat and went on to describe the tannat wine as being, "Unique and 100% tannat, which is rare as it's usually a blending grape, meaning a small portion is added to other wine to make it more dry on the palate at the end of the sip. It's also notably the only wine varietal that's a palindrome — it's spelled the same forwards and backwards. I hope you like it!" as she then walked away from the table and headed back into the tasting room.

MIXOLOGIST

B etty is a mixologist. She not only made that frosé a while back, she made a beverage she could drink all day and not get drunk from. It was the perfect remedy for working at a social place, and even hanging out on her day off at, as this is where her friends all hung out too.

The wine was made into a modified version of the winery's frosé wine by combining it with seltzer. We sold the seltzer in the tasting room for those who were designated drivers or under age 21, so we have cases of the stuff. The seltzer water came in different flavors and she particularly like the peach flavor. She mixed it with the rosé wine. This mixture can be varied to control one's alcohol, and adds a hydration element to her drink. Maybe she made it 50% each seltzer and wine, and other times I only saw her add what she called "a floater" of rosé to the top of the seltzer. Her genius leadership strikes again, and it's a winning combination that to this day I sometimes copy at home and at my book club meetings when I want to have a little wine, but not get tipsy. Genius, thank you Betty!

Speaking of creativity, I was pretty creative when making something pretty. I always putzed with the flowers and greenery in the tasting room. Betty saw this behavior time and time again. She asked me if I would want to teach a crafting class event at the winery. I was so honored that my pruning was not only helping the health of the indoor plants but also helping this opportunity for myself and my future students come to fruition. This started at Celestial Cellars with planning a pumpkin succulent craft session in Fall, and then later with a holiday wreath making class. While I love being in front of a class of students doing crafty things, I love an early bedtime, too. This daytime creative gig was perfect for me, as it was mid-day Betty sure knew how to pick the right people for the job. She picked Sharon who'd stand up to fake people and me to do the flowers.

PERK

In summertime at Celestial Cellars, there's live music every weekend. On Saturdays there's an acoustic artist, and on Sundays a band of different genres from week to week. When there's a band like this, we tend to get lots of customers. We charged a $5 entry fee, like a cover fee, which helps keep people just wanting a free afternoon out of the tasting room. We're pretty lenient on letting the band members partners in for free and we also let the wine club members in for free too. It's such a great perk of the wine club membership if you think about it. You're basically treated like family from the moment you sign up. These busy weekends call for a second bar, one that's closer to the patrons and all the happenings, so we have two large bar carts on wheels in the backyard area. They're both fully stocked with the tasting menu's large offerings, and we have access to the frosé machine as well. The cool part of this bar, is it's the best view of the back yard and the stage, so many times it feels like you're at the concert too. We get to chit chat with our coworkers and customers come up to us to order their drinks. The only challenging part of this is the fact that our iPads are further from the internet modem.

PET PEEVE

Like most Millennials, I love good pun, but wearing a tee shirt that says, "red, white and blue" alongside three cartoony wine glasses with red, white and blue color wine in the glass is an ick. I loved having opinions about winery clothing now as I had been such an observer in the past. I felt experienced enough to have opinions and to know better. A shirt that says, "red, white and blue" screams only one of two things to your wine educator. Neither is good. When we see that shirt, we think either, *I hope they used Kohl's Cash on that ugly thing* or we question your knowledge about wine and think, *They know there's no blue wine, right?* Basically, it's fugly (freaking ugly) and is embarrassing. Plus, it makes us, and others, question why you thought you needed to bring that home and wear in public. Even if the person who gave it to you is with you wine tasting, don't wear it. Even if it's fourth of July, don't wear it. If it was a gift, tell the gift giver that you love it so much and that you don't want to risk ruining it with a wine spill today and then subsequently don't wear it. If you do find a blue wine: 1. Don't drink it, and 2. Still don't wear the shirt. Oh, and even if you made it with your own Cricut crafting machine, and think you made it *better* than the original one you saw at Kohls, it's still tacky. There's something so cheesy about it and makes you stick out so much in the fancy wine setting. It takes the cheesy matching shirt with your partner that extra step too far.

BARTENDER

O ne afternoon four people came to the winery. One of the new coworker girls, the type who never stayed long enough for their name to matter to me, sat them at a four top. This is a restaurant term for a table for four people. At the table, they were given our large folding menus and while it was sunny out, enjoyed the shade from a tree nearby mixed with the umbrella. The table was within sight distance from the tasting room. This is a preferred place to seat customers, so we can see how full their glasses are, so we know when to approach the table with the bottle of the next wine they're going to be served next. We can watch once they get to the red wine. Before that, the white wines on the menu look pretty clear even to the most eagle-eyed of us Tasting Room Associates. When they're on the white wines, the rule of thumb is to give them 10 minutes to enjoy the taste before going out to refill their glass and teach them about this new wine. The group seemed to be a family as there was two people in their 40's or 50's and one teenager, and one young 20's looking. I thought they were such a quin-tessential nuclear family and thought it nice that the folks could enjoy an afternoon picnicking with their kiddos. I approached the table, as it was decided inside amongst the workers that I would pour for them. They were seated further from the tasting room, up on a slight hill. This gave them a wonderful view of the malbec vines growing near the tasting room and sat them in the middle of nature. They were under a canopy of trees and on the rough-cut tanbark, also known as mulch, beneath their feet. As I walked up the hill to their table, I tripped on my own shoe as a piece of the bank made its way between my foot and the sandal. Note taken: do not wear open-toed shoes to work. Getting back to the scene, I approached the table with the Rhone style white wine, and had my speech all prepared. I knew I'd point out the varietals included in the wine, and explain how the weather in Paso mimics the weather in the Rhone valley, allowing us to grow these white wine grapes to perfection. I would also mention how the wine was so well-received and earned a 94 Points review in Wine Enthusiast magazine for two years in a row. But my trip literally tripped my mind up and when I got to the table I was a bit flustered. The dad figure at the table saw my discombobulation and said, "It's okay, I was a bartender too!" and continued saying how they'd like to order two of the meat and cheese platters and two full wine tastings as well as two sodas. This is when it really felt different to me. People were asking for various drinks and food to be brought to their table. This was such a different vibe from the convivial winery bar situation, but I didn't object. I just noticed the differences. I went inside and made a tray to carry these requests to the people. I made sure to walk much more carefully, too. When it was time for them to pay, I did notice their generous tip was similar to table service restaurants too — a nice 20% added to their tab. I thought to myself, *Hmm, I could certainly get used to this change in procedures.* And my second bit of work for this table began. I brought the same tray out to the table after they left and bussed it like they do in a restaurant. I added the cans and trays the charcuterie came on to the recycle bins, and added the glasses to the dishwasher for cleaning. I then returned to the table to wipe it down and prepare for the next customer. It was like nothing even happened, besides getting my steps in, and an instant gratification,

PROLLY DON'T WANT A CRACKER

Finishing up his break which he took in the kitchen area, Josh came into the tasting room as he heard a noise coming from an animal of some sort. Josh wiped the crumbs off his shirt and walked into the tasting room bar area to see a customer dressed in cargo shorts and a neon green t-shirt. On the man's left shoulder was a large white parrot. The man asks Josh, "Got any crackers?" Never skipping a beat, Josh asks, "Your bird named Polly, by chance?" The two men chuckle and it's like they've been friends for years. The parrot definitely helps break through small talk, I notice! Josh begins his customer service spiel and asks if the man would like to try our tasting flight. But adds a line about, "Hope it's the only flight that takes place at his bar today." By the time the chardonnay is poured, I hear the man ask for nuts or snack mix or water cups or something else at the bar here like other places. Josh smiles and says, "Well, ya know, pairing crackers or water with wine tasting flights is quite controversial among different tasting rooms. Some believe that the flight, order of the wine tasting sips, is perfectly designed, and the water and crackers change the mouthfeel of the wine. Snack mix is so delicious man, I understand you on that, but we don't do that here. I've heard some other tasting rooms serve crackers at the bar. We all do things a little different around here in Paso."

The parrot man said, "It's alright man, I'm just joshing you. I'm more of a beer guy, you can probably guess."

"There's definitely some things we all agree on!" Josh

exuberantly says and adds, "That's a whole other thing up here man. We have lots of breweries and distilleries too. I love it here. But dang have you noticed how many glasses we go through here? At least my hands fit in pint glasses or wine glasses. I'd hate to polish those snifter glasses all day long."

Bird daddy replied, "There's a lot of rules up here with etiquette and shit, right?" Josh sighs and says, "Kinda man, it's true. Especially when it comes to the glass and sipping. Fist you'll want to hold the stem of the glass, smell the wine, take a small sip, close your eyes and savor, open eyes and sip again, swirl the glass to see the color, and if they're any 'legs' on the glass, those are due to the sugar content in the juice, and after regarding its characteristics, sip again, savor again. It's a lot, I admit, but it's like they say, 'Wine is grown in the most beautiful places in the world. If it's ugly there, they likely make beer.'" The two men share a laugh that is loud and makes the bird reach out its wings and bob its head a little. Bird daddy says, "And that must be true because, to me, the best beer is from Colorado and Wisconsin, but I wouldn't ever go to a winery there!"

FORTY TWO

Autumn Harvest is the plants' time to shine. It's when the fruit is the plumpest and ready to pick because the sugar content, called Brix, determines the potential alcohol content. During this time the leaves change color after the grapes are picked, leaves fall and this mulch is like a vitamin and ground-cover for the soil. At Celestial Cellars, the owner was discussing wine harvest time being delayed because of weather. You see, the harvest often happens in September, but the exact date depends on when the grapes are fully ripe.

Unlike the harvest, Adrian and I had set a date. It was to be on September 4th where we would capitalize on the three-day weekend for Labor Day and allow for more guests to attend. As many were traveling to celebrate with us, they had more time to travel to the ceremony location. Just like Adrian's nature leads him to be happy with uncomplicated needs for fulfillment, I, too, wanted a small wedding. We made a guest list and added up the people. When we saw the number, it felt too perfect. It was a reference to Douglas Adams' Hitchhikers' Guide to the Galaxy's character Deep Thought's explanation of the meaning of life — 42.

We organized our wedding into an entire weekend which began with a Welcome Pool Party the day before the wedding itself. Leaning into our German heritage, we had Beda's Bier-garden cater traditional German food, pig roast and all. With the wedding festivities being in our newly bought home in Atas-cadero, we used the home as an AirBnB and hosted guests who had travelled far to be with us. With it being a backyard wedding, we wanted to enjoy the neighborhood vibe and had Negranti Creamery Ice Cream truck deliver ice cream sandwiches. A local band, The Belmonts, a husband-and-wife duo, performed their twist on Taylor Swift's song Love Story, per our request. To signify this wedding being a uniting of a family, and not just us as a couple, a moment after my husband and I exchanged rings, he gifted my son a necklace. It was made from LEGO bricks where the two rectangles clicked together to make a heart, symbolizing our family clicking into a place of love.

LOVED

Despite Josh's first-hand ranch experience, when attending parties, he channels his chef mom's influences and brings a local and fresh offering to the Celestial Cellars Christmas party. He brought a large fresh ahi and edamame salad that was delectable with the vintage champagne served. This fresh food paired so well with crisp winter.

Winter is the dormant cycle of the vineyard. This makes it not the conventionally prettiest time because it's after the harvest and the vines look like sticks growing out of the earth. It's also dormant — like in that it's also when tourism to the tasting room is the slowest. It's during this quiescent time, that the wine tasting room and vineyards feel different. It's slow and cozy. It's also when things are indoorsy, yet also proves growth is happening even in winter in order for Springtime to bloom.

This winter, I loved being able to attend the winery staff Christmas party with Adrian as my new husband. Actual husband. I loved saying that word. Husband. I loved that we wore wedding bands that we exchanged in front of friends and family. I loved the relationship he was building with my son over LEGOS and Taylor Swift's music. Adrian adores me. He tells me my presence upgrades his purpose. He says I'm the best investment he'll ever make. This makes me feel I am safe and I know I am ready for all sides of me to me loved.

He shows up for me in many areas of our lives. Adrian's character allows him to stay in love even when it's hard. His touch became medicine. He softened the edge of things that still hurt me. My energy felt different. I was more centered feeling than even after attending a yoga class or sound bath. I was more sensitive to the energy of those around me. I couldn't stand inauthentic or negative energy. My intuition sharpened. I distanced myself from things that disrupted my peace.

It's often said that commitment, maturity, and the ability to endure life's ugly parts is what sustains a marriage. I listened to the advice I had heard that says it's best to marry your best friend. Better yet, I married my friend's husband's best friend. He's the one with whom I never run out of things to say. The one who speaks highly of me. Who always gives me the benefit of the doubt. The one I can be myself with. Even the weird sides of myself. I love his weird side too. Our love doesn't have to be grand. It shows its finest self in the small gestures, like looking outside when one of us points out how the twilight light is making the hills do that pretty thing again.

DRY JANUARY OR TRY JANUARY

There's a philosophy about the beginning of the year being the perfect time to change oneself for the better. For many struggling with alcohol, or even those who are sober curious, having a dry January means not drinking any kind of alcohol during the month of January. I first learned about this when a customer said that he was the designated driver for the group today as he was "having a dry January after drinking far too much in December." He said they're paying for his snacks today, and would like to purchase a charcuterie tray to pick on. His friend leaned over, and explained with enthusiasm, "He's having a Dry January and I'm having a Try January! Let me try the rosé!" with so much laughter the table next to them looked over to see what the joke they missed was. Despite the differences in philosophies, it does seem their friendship was a match made in heaven. One could taste wine and do so safely with a personal, and well-fed, driver.

XOXO, SANTA

A customer pair was assigned to me and seated inside the bar on the high-top table. They had a moment of pause before getting up on the tall chairs, but made it safely. They mentioned how they would rather stay inside today as it was too warm for them outside. They shared that they were visiting from "up north" to which I assumed meant the Bay Area someplace, but I got distracted with answering a phone call the tasting room got, so I didn't follow up where they were visiting us from.

They were in their 60's and were pretty non-descript but gave off a homey, friendly feeling and look that one has when they definitely know how to cook, and probably have quilting skills to boot. They selected a variety of wines after revisiting, which means retasting, the wines. This meant they got many more sips than the customary tasting, as their revisits indicated they were serious wine buyers. They liked many of our wines, and bought two cases. They got 6 bottles of four different wines to make up their 24 bottles, and even asked for a glass of wine each to sit and drink now. I packaged everything up for them with a smile, despite being a bit fatigued from running back and forth to the cellar as their minds were changing about their selection. At the end of their time with us, we settled up their tab. Thankfully my iPad was working wonderfully as we were close to the wifi as they sat inside. I handed them the iPad and used my favorite line, "A tip is never expected, but always appreciated." After signing for his credit card transaction, he reached into his pocket, and handed me a white and red sticker with a picture of a cartoon

Santa's face on it. As he handed it to me, he said, "Here's your tip. Now you can say you served Santa!" while he smiled and chuckled.

I laughed to myself, *They're from up north...they must have meant really far up north- The North Pole!* And thought that it's good I offered to walk their cases of wine out to their car, or else I may have gotten coal. After returning from delivering the cases to their car, Betty saw me staring at the small round sticker, and I told her, "This is my tip from Santa." To which she replied, "Of course it is, Ms. Christmas!," bringing up the old nickname she gave me at Stonefruit Canyon and shook her head in a knowing way that actual cash money would've been nicer. This sort of thing had happened to her too, so she understood that some customers are just like that and she retreated into the employees only doorway and into the backroom office area.

HEAT

W hen romanticized, wine is called a time capsule in a bottle. It should be treated as inherently precious out of respect for all that went into making it and to preserve its integrity so you can enjoy it when you're ready. While it needs warm climates to grow, after its bottled, wine doesn't like to be stored in sun or heat. Paso's warm climate is sometimes a surprise to people. Sometimes people to come to Paso don't realize just how warm it can get here in the Summertime and throughout the Fall. These warm-weather visitors come to Paso, go to a winery, buy wine and put the bottles or cases, in their trunks. They then go to another winery, and do the same. Stocking their trunk full of time-capsuled treasures from their day of wine tasting. The problem with this is that cars get hot in the heat, and with them leaving their bottles in the car's trunk during summertime trips, the heat makes the glass get warm, and after even more time in the heat, the fermentation inside the bottle makes pressure in the bottle, but the real issue is when there's pressure on the cork. All this pressure can make the wine explode out of the bottle and all over your car's trunk. This happens in the late afternoon after collecting bottles all day. When it happens, customers are so surprised. However, it's not really a surprise to us in the tasting room, and to deal with it and help as much as we can, we have a big bottle of Wine Away, a fabric treatment spray, for when red wine comes in contact with porous fabrics. However effective Wine Away is, it's best to avoid having a wine explosion by bringing your purchased wine to your hotel room mid-day where it would be in a better temperature-controlled environment until you can bring it home and put it in your cellar, wine fridge, or even a cold garage until it's ready to be enjoyed.

WINE FRIDGE

As people's collection and proclivity to buy wine to store it for future enjoyment grows, so has the business of at-home wine refrigerators. These are a great way to upgrade the bottle from being on the countertop or in a box in the garage storage. Prices range from $200 for a small one, up to $1,500 for a big 300-bottle refrigerator. I needed to learn this as Adrian and I needed to set up and organize a fridge for the collection of wine I sold him when he was trying to make the tasting room manager happy he was lingering for hours.

When researching wine fridges, we learned some are dual-zone, meaning one area is known to be a certain degree and the other section at another degree, as expected. That's the easier, more self-explanatory kind as the zones represent which wine goes in each area. If you have a fridge with one temp zone, there's unofficial temp zones you can take advantage of. Meaning, one option is to recognize where the cooling element is (it's often on the top, bottom or back) and align the varietals accordingly. Specifically, white wine is best stored in the range of 43-55 degrees Fahrenheit and red wine varietals at 55 to 64 degrees Fahrenheit. By placing the white wine on the bottom of the fridge, if that's where the cooling element is, it ensures the coolest area of the fridge is hitting the wine that requires such temps. This little wine fridge hack is just the starter knowledge about how to organize them. Some members in the Paso Robles Wine Fanatics Facebook group mentioned organizing by varietal and even the option to organize by "drinkability" meaning one shelf of things you want to drink soon, and another shelf of wine you intend to store for a certain year, or occasion, for example. Clearly, there are many ways to approach something.

PROFESSIONAL PARTY PERSON

Since he's a bit of a local celebrity, when radio guy Alex Hill goes places, people pay attention. He once credited Stonefruit Canyon with being revolutionary. The culture here is revolutionary. The owners of Stonefruit Canyon came to the 30-year anniversary party for Celestial Cellars. That's pretty special that they can recognize each other's craft and function without competition. Alex truly loves the heritage of Paso, and when he points out things like that, he makes loving Paso easy for others too. He said, "The people of Paso are a special ingredient to what makes this work the way it does." He follows up with explaining there's open arms here. It begins with the sharing of wine equipment is something that happens all over Paso. I'd have to agree with Alex. This young wine region can skyrocket in an environment of teamwork. It's welcoming to each other and is also welcoming for people to come here as tourists. There's enough to go around. Everyone can experience the kind generosity while traveling here to taste wine and enjoy the scenic county. They can feel the kind heartbeat of the place.

Speaking of sharing, Celestial Cellars has a production facility they share with other wineries, I can see how this mutual success helped fuel their own winery and make connections with others. If one winery succeeded, then Paso succeeds at the same time as they grow together. So many wineries that you pass on the way to and from Paso are newer and the Heck and Bergheart families truly are as pioneers here. They embody people helping each other. As I listened to this radio show, and met him again, it felt good to work for a family like this, in a situation like this. They're all pioneers, but also incredibly welcoming and helpful. I felt a sense of pride to be part of this wine world in Paso.

I had the opportunity to pour wine for Alex one evening. When presented with the huge menu he chose to start his visit off with a refreshing frosé as it was a warm afternoon in the backyard. The second time he came to the bar, I had the chance to pour for him again. I was so tickled that he chose my favorite wine at Celestial Cellars was making at the time — the grenache. Ours was made 100% grenache. This bottle was single-varietal, but it's often paired with syrah and mourvèdre. One sniff and sip and it would burst in your face with plum and raspberry notes. They really are so delicious here, and this grenache was no exception. It was just how I wanted to feel. It's fun, light, and perky with an outstanding quality. It embodies the Central Coast's take on the iconic French Rhone blend. I noticed that Alex's choices are also my go-to's and I felt connected to his palate's preferences. I tucked this info away as it may be useful one day. Like for example if on his radio show he recommended something else in the area, I would know we share a similar palate preference and would likely enjoy that too.

CHEERS!

My time at Celestial Cellars came to an end like a beautifully wrapped gift, just the way I like it. I decided to celebrate my last day at the winery with their 30th-anniversary party. The tasting room was up for sale, and the owner had a vision for the winery to become smaller. They wanted to focus on their own production harvests and reduce the variety of wines they offered. And guess what? The Anniversary party was a real party! There was a band, food trucks, and so many lovely fans, wine club members, and even Paso royalty, the Heck Family, were there. People were dancing, making out, and enjoying the music. As the sun began to set, it felt like the end of an era, just like the end of my time in Paso.

My experience at wineries really sparked my interest in wine. I went on to take two courses at the Napa Valley Wine Academy and passed the WSET Level 1 and 2 awards in wine. As I look back on my journey, I'm amazed by how much I've grown and evolved. Just like vines go through cycles of growth and rebirth, we too are different every day and capable of growth, no matter what challenges we face. With hard work, we're all headed to bloom and grow like the vines in Paso's wine region.

When the sun rose again, I saw things differently than when I first started this industry. I've learned that my value isn't based on how productive I am. I'm worthy just the way I am. Now, I make choices that honor my needs, values, and well-being. Rebuilding my self-esteem has made me more confident in taking care of myself and others. This wasn't something that happened by chance. I was bold enough to build it, scared enough to care, and relentless enough to finish it.

Andy Reiff, a director and costume designer from New York, once said, "I knew something exciting was waiting for me if I let go of the fear of judgment." Even during tough times, I've always been brave enough to try new things. Living in California's Central Coast, I am surrounded by hundreds of vineyards. It's a beautiful place for the senses, and it has a magical way of changing people and visitors. In this lovely setting, I've been on a journey of self-discovery, and it's helped me become the best version of myself.

I've had many ups and downs in my life, but I've always believed that the most beautiful moments happen during transitions. Just like diurnal animals that are most active during sunrise and sunset, I find that the most meaningful moments in life are the ones that involve change. It's like we're rewarded for embracing the transition with a view of a beautiful sky. I've realized that all these fleeting moments in life have come together to make a memorable experience. I'm so grateful for this journey, and the fact I have now become a Cat Lady thanks to the musings of the winery cats I had the pleasure to work for, I mean with. It's said the romance in wine is all about drinking it. I'll end this on a high note, just like the best drinks start and end with, a big "Cheers!"

AFTER THE LAST SIP

Bringing more fiction to the aspects of this work of Autobiographical Fiction, here's my prediction of what's next for those who brought Main Character energy to the tasting rooms:

Josh planted grapevines in his modest home set within ample acreage in San Miguel, just north of Paso Robles. Using all the helpful connections he made in this industry; he bottles about 100 cases in a typical year. He specializes in the renegade wine blends that Paso encourages. To his partner, his jokes never get old. The older woman is he dating is so impressed with all he's accomplished in his life so far. He is still charming as ever.

Sharon became a running coach and Big Sister with Big Sisters of America as she connected with kiddos and their dark moods. She inspired children who have been through a lot to overcome a lot using her holistic approach — run it off!

Riley works on Capitol Hill. For the senate, she is an aide who is heading up the committee for LGBTQA+ activism. She feels like the luckiest woman in the world to be married to the sexiest Belizean-American. They share their home with two rescue dogs and made a pact to add at least two stamps to their passport annually.

Betty started a company called, Human Resources Paso, which is a recruitment company matching people's talents to their best jobs. She found love in adopting a brute dog who wears a diamond necklace which her husband, an up-and-coming R&B singer, got them matching ones. Her and her loving partner bonded over weight loss, tattoos, and their newfound love of pickleball.

Ambrose lives near the site of the Woodstock festival in upstate New York and combines his California cool with East Coast prep. He manages his online rare bookstore and he and his baby mama have taken on a romantic third, a dark-haired woman who designs storefronts for holidays. Living as a throuple, they believe in pairing chardonnay with French fries.

Henry is probably still fixing a fountain in his yard, and drinking a local Malbec, but since he hasn't figured out his iPhone enough to return the author's calls or text messages, we will never really know what he's up to nowadays.

Adrian and Jenn enjoyed a honeymoon to Paris France, just as he predicted they would when chatting with customers at Stonefruit Canyon years ago. In Paris' 16th arrondissement, they lived like locals in their friend's apartment. They toured around Paris by foot, Metro, and even in a classic Peugeot. They took a day trip to Disneyland Paris, as well as one to the Champagne region where they took a sensory tour of the Veuve Clicquot champagne house. After all, they would need some champagne as they would have a lot to celebrate in their life together. While dining out for an exquisite New Year's Eve dinner, with Ian at Somm's Kitchen in Paso, Jenn shared how the two of them met and were told in return, "Now that's the story of the day!" This comment inspired her to go through her notes and get the stories down in Word to share her favorite wine-drenched love story.

BOOK CLUB QUESTIONS

To get the group discussion going, here's some questions to use during your book club meeting about Tasting Room Confidential. The author may be available to FaceTime or Skype with your book club.

To inquire, reach out to her via email JenniferLuckMuller@gmail.com

1. How does Jenn's self-image evolve throughout the novel?

2. When Josh invites all the workers out for appetizers after work one night, and only Jenn shows, do you think Josh really invited others, or was it a ploy to go on a date?

3. Thinking about the scenes where clothes, shoes and accessories are discussed, what roles does clothing play in the novel?

4. Do you think the story will inspire other profession confidential books, for example "Hair Salon Confidential" or "Mail Room Confidential," and if so, what would you like to read about?

. . .

5. Did the novel help you appreciate wine and winery tasting rooms more, or less? If so, how will your next reservation be different?

6. If there was a sequel, staring one of the characters other than our Narrator Jenn, who would you want to star in it?

7. How comfortable are you touring wineries now? Do they sound more fun, or in what ways will you see them differently now?

8. What's your favorite memories from touring wineries? Was it the wine, or something they do for the guests that make the experience memorable?

9. If you were to take a leap and explore a new career path, what would it be? Is there a job idea that got away?

10. Were you Team Josh or Team Adrian?